LEE KINGMAN is the author of the much-acclaimed *The Year of the Raccoon*, which was selected a Notable Book by the American Library Association. In private life she is Mrs. Robert Natti, and the mother of two college-age children. A native of Reading, Massachusetts, she was graduated from Colby Junior College and Smith College, and currently lives with her husband on Cape Ann.

THE LAUREL-LEAF LIBRARY brings together under a single imprint outstanding works of fiction and nonfiction particularly suitable for young adult readers, both in and out of the classroom. This series is under the editorship of M. Jerry Weiss, Distinguished Professor of Communications, Jersey City State College, and Charles F. Reasoner, Associate Professor, Elementary Education, New York University.

D1715511

The Peter Pan Bag

by Lee Kingman

Published by
Dell Publishing Co., Inc.
750 Third Avenue, New York, N. Y. 10017

Laurel-Leaf Library ® TM 766734,
Dell Publishing Co., Inc.
Reprinted by arrangement with Houghton Mifflin Company,
Boston, Massachusetts
Printed in the United States of America
First Laurel printing—February 1971
Second Laurel printing—March 1971
Third Laurel printing—June 1971

The
Peter Pan
Bag

1

"YOU'RE THE ONLY ONE in this whole family, O'Casey, who hasn't bared his teeth and growled at me since I came home." Wendy lay on the living-room rug. She stretched out an arm and hugged O'Casey, her long dark hair falling over his red head. "The only one who hasn't treated me like a dog is you, dog."

The Irish setter gave her a patient look, but he threw off her hug and scratched himself violently. Wendy hunched away from him. "Don't look at me as if I'd given you the itch either. That's the way Mum and Dad look. As if I'd broken out suddenly with scrofula. And what have I done? Just told the truth about things. Just tried to get through to them where things are at."

A log glowed in the fireplace, dimming and brightening like a neon sign as the June storm fussed down the chimney. Two days of rain and wind forced a chill through the house, just as it forced the Allardyce family inside to stare unwillingly at each other.

"What's gotten into us!" Mrs. Allardyce had exclaimed at the supper table after scolding Dougal for a sharp remark that caused an insurrection on his younger brother Ian's part. "You used to love storms around this house. You reveled in feeling besieged and made up all kinds of games. I can remember, only three years ago, when you spent hours in the attic making medieval costumes, so you could defend the castle the next time we were stormed in."

"Mum—three years ago we were little kids!" Annetta interrupted.

"I know your interests have changed," said Mrs. Allardyce, "but it's sad. All we have is an atmosphere of bad tempers. What's happened to us?"

"For one thing, we can't be put off with foolish games any more," explained Wendy. "Even if Father's idea of a great evening is a two-hour game of I-Doubt-It or Hide-and-Seek. Being *en masse* as a family isn't our idea of a good time. Home is just not the center of our lives, and you ought to understand that by now. I'd like to be anywhere but here."

"That's very obvious," said Mr. Allardyce.

"And logical for seventeen," admitted Mrs. Allardyce, smiling reminiscently.

"And for fifteen, too!" Rosalyn reminded them, shaking her head in such vigorous agreement that her long black hair snapped about.

"Then since you're such logical parents who understand what I want," said Wendy in a voice frigid with sarcasm, "what is wrong with letting me carry out the plans I made for this summer with Miggle? I promised her I'd be there tomorrow."

"Three very simple things are wrong." Her father didn't raise his voice even though the wind whipped the rain gustily against the windows. "One. You made your plans with Miss Margaret Lou Banbury without once consulting your parents for their permission— which was impractical of you, at best. Two, we do not know the Banburys except just meeting them during Parents' Weekend at Parsley Hall. My impression was their views as parents differed extensively from ours."

"Does that make your views more right than theirs?" Wendy asked.

"A clever interjection, my girl. But I will not be thrown off the point—which is that they differ, and I believe I am right. And three, you may not spend the summer in New York City at the Banburys' apartment alone with Miggle."

"But I'm to keep her company so she can stay there! If I can't come, they'll make her go to her grandmother's in exile."

"Exile?" asked her mother.

"Northeast Harbor. Way up in Maine."

"But that's marvelous country to be exiled in!" Mrs. Allardyce exclaimed. "I spent a summer there when I was fifteen. I adored it."

"Fifteen in your youth, Mother, is equivalent to about age eleven today. Absolutely unformed and inept."

Dougal rose and bowed. "How do you do, everyone. I'm eleven. I'm unformed and inept."

Annetta, smugly thirteen, laughed.

Wendy ignored them. "It is exile. Miggle says it's nothing but ice water to swim in and innocent, boring boys who love to sail and play tennis and climb rocks."

"How I wish we had some boys who liked to sail and play tennis and climb rocks around here then," said Mrs. Allardyce.

"They are equally boring here," insisted Wendy. "Except that the boys in this village are concerned with the insides of their souped-up cars, and the boys at the high school are a bunch of weightlifters."

"Those sound like healthy avocations," Mr. Allardyce said calmly.

"Too healthy for words. Look, you're paying good money to send Rosalyn and me off to Parsley Hall for our education, because the high school here is so limited. So we don't really have friends here anymore. Not since grammar school."

"Don't you ever see any of the girls you played with then?"

Wendy shrugged. "Mum, half those girls are either going to hairdresser's school—or married."

"Married! At seventeen?"

"Or eighteen. And half of them married because they had to, I'll bet," Rosalyn added.

"Really, Rosalyn. You are exaggerating."

"*Au contraire*, I'm being quite statistical. Do you really want us to renew our acquaintance with our local peers?"

"Rosalyn, your tone of voice in speaking to your mother could be infinitely kinder." Mr. Allardyce frowned.

"Well, you've brought us up to look at facts and be honest," Wendy protested. "We're just telling you the facts. We don't have friends here anymore. This may be an old country house, but this isn't summer-resort territory, either. No summer people. No winter friends. There's absolutely nothing here but us and the mosquitoes."

"What's wrong with us, except you?" Ian asked in a most innocent tone. "I thought you loved it here, Wendy! I thought you loved the apple-jungle and the tree house and the pirate boat in the creek and the secret letters. You swore once, like Peter Pan, remember? There's still a secret-letter oath you wrote down and stuck under the shingles on the side of the house that says, 'I won't grow up. I swear it by the light of Tinkerbelle and the shadow of Peter Pan.' And it's signed Wendy Allardyce, in blood."

"I did love it here," said Wendy, "when I was a child. When I was little enough to think the gnarly bunch of trees in that leftover orchard was an apple-jungle, and I was little enough so I had to climb up to see the tree house, and little enough so I could fit in that dinghy in the creek. But look at me! Really look! I'm not little anymore."

Wendy rose dramatically. Inside she was begging her parents to see her anew—as Wendy Allardyce, that vibrant, energetic, logical protestor of the archaic views of her parents' youth.

But with a sinking heart she was sure her mother's mind read like a news release to the paper about "the lovely and competent Miss Wendy Allardyce, who next year will be a senior at Parsley Hall. Undoubtedly she will be a finalist for a National Merit Scholarship, and she will be admitted to the college of her choice. She is a member of the Student Judicial Board and this past year was responsible for organizing a petition to allow boys to visit the campus every weekend instead of on Stated Festive Occasions."

To which Wendy would have added a disgusted footnote: the petition was acclaimed as a reasonable presentation on behalf of current student thought but filed in a large cabinet in the dean's office.

"Miss Allardyce is an accomplished lute player, who often accompanies the Parsley Hall Madri-Gals. She will be particularly remembered for her stunning performance as Wendy (typecasting, anyone?) in last year's Graduation Week performance of *Peter Pan*."

Her father's voice, as he lovingly said, "Oh, Wendy, baby!" confirmed it. It was just the way he greeted her as she came off stage at the end of the play. "Oh, Wendy, baby!" As if he couldn't believe all the talent and delight radiating from his incredible daughter.

"Look at me now, please!" begged Wendy. "Can't you see—I've grown up?"

She stared around the table—at her mother, head tipped to one side, happily appraising the charming girl before her and her store of college prospects and eventual marriageable qualities; at her father, beaming with love and admiration; at Rosalyn, who was about to toss her crumpled napkin onto the table and arise to say, "Me, too"; at Annetta, eyes sparkling at the scene. At Dougal, chewing. At Ian, puzzled—waiting to see if this were beginning one of the fantastic games Wendy used to make up.

"Don't look at me like that! It's a trap." Wendy stamped her foot so hard her toes tingled and her heel hurt. She banged her hand on the table—and the lights went out.

"Oh, I hate this family!" she cried in the dark. "Whenever you try to come down to the nitty-gritty, everything goes anticlimactic, and we end up in the dark again."

"That makes us very symbolic!" Annetta shrieked happily.

"*Nitty-gritty*." Mrs. Allardyce wondered over the words. "Sounds like knitting with unscoured wool or weaving potholders out of barbwire."

"You have the most ridiculous mind, Mother," said Wendy. "It's a word that came out of the ghetto. It means the—well, the *nub* of everything."

"The gut issue," Rosalyn added.

"Why not just say 'guts' then?" asked Dougal.

"Why don't we see what we can do about the lights?" Ian asked impatiently.

"I'll tell you what's wrong with this family," Annetta announced. "We discuss things too much. Do you know any other family that sits discussing something instead of fixing the fuse? Daddy, don't you know about fuses?"

"Of course I know about fuses. But I had a feeling we were about to illuminate something more important."

"Don't bother being symbolic, Father!" said Wendy. "This family is not only an anachronism. It's like a great big invisible net. It's why I want to get away from us this summer. I can't stand this intellectual discussing all the time. It's like Chekov's plays—with everyone planning what he will do and talking it to death. It's so simple, I just want to go out—and *do*."

"Do what?" asked Mrs. Allardyce practically.

Mr. Allardyce pushed his heavy oak chair away from the table and settled comfortably. "Your statement contains so many elements. Let's take them one at a time, Wendy."

"Dougal, do you know where my flashlight is?" asked Ian.

"There's only one element!" Wendy insisted. "I've got to *go.*"

Annetta burst into laughter. "Does that remind anyone of our camping trip on Cape Breton? With Wendy begging at every curve for Daddy to stop and let her dash for the bushes? And Daddy looking at the drop over the cliffs and saying, 'Let the pressure build!' "

"I don't know where your flashlight is, Ian."

"Annetta, I am not amused," said Wendy.

"No. That's been your problem lately," said Annetta.

"I remember now, Ian. You took the batteries out of your flashlight to use in my computer."

"Wendy, what do you mean this family is an anachronism?" asked her mother anxiously.

"And kindly explain your simile that this family is like a great big invisible net!" Mr. Allardyce couldn't be seen in the dark room. But his presence in the chair seemed heavier and larger than life.

"I don't think we have intellectual discussions all the time," objected Rosalyn. "I think some of our topics are rather disgusting for dinner conversation. I didn't think the Cape Breton trip was funny, either."

"But where did I leave the shell of the flashlight, Dougal?"

"I meant—oh, will people hush and listen!" Wendy cried out. "This family is nothing but a Tower of Babble."

"Babel," Dougal corrected. "Ian, I think the shell of your flashlight is on the windowsill in our bathroom."

"Good," said Ian. "I know where the fuses are."

The boys pushed back their chairs and rose in the dark.

"You have not been dismissed from the table," said Mr. Allardyce.

"Don't you want us to fix the fuse?"

"When you have been dismissed. We are having a family discussion.

"But I don't want to be a family discussion!" Wendy pleaded. "You're cruel. I just want to be—me."

"Richard—" said Mrs. Allardyce softly.

"All right. Boys, please see to the lights. If it proves not to be a fuse, call me. The wiring in the house is rather exotic."

The boys felt for their silver napkin rings and rolled up their napkins. They placed their chairs neatly at the table and stepped cautiously toward the door.

"That's what I mean about our family being an anachronism," said Wendy. "Do you know another family where the father doesn't commute to work? Ours works at home. And where they use silver napkin rings and the kids have to wait to be excused from the table? *We're unreal!*"

"I don't see anything unrealistic about good manners," gasped Mrs. Allardyce.

"Those are details," said Mr. Allardyce. "Let's get at the important thing. Your riddle, Wendy. Why is the Allardyce family like a great big invisible net?"

"Because you've let us poke our heads out of the interstices—"

"Oh, impressive word!" cried Annetta. "No wonder you can do the *New York Times* crossword puzzles."

"Annetta, be still," warned Mrs. Allardyce.

Wendy marched verbally on. "All right—you've let us see out in all directions, pretending we are free to learn and question and think and do. You've always encouraged us to express ourselves. But now, when I want to go away and *do* my own thing, I discover that the clear space, the pretended freedom, isn't big enough for me to step through. There are the ropes, suddenly visible, framing my only view, and I am a prisoner."

"Wendy!" Rosalyn exclaimed. "If you'd only declaimed like that in speech class, you'd have won the Elsie L. Fribble Prize!"

"Rosalyn, you be still," said Mrs. Allardyce.

"And what is *your own thing*, as you so quaintly phrase it?" asked Mr. Allardyce.

"I don't know." Wendy's voice broke. "And it's not a quaint phrase I made up. It's a very real statement of the times, if you'd just listen to our everyday conversation once in a while. But whatever my own thing is, I know I can't find it here. I have to find it somewhere else—by myself. Are you going to deny me the inherent right to find myself?"

"What an effect the dark has!" exclaimed Mrs. Allardyce. "It makes every sentence so portentous. So full of mystery and omen."

"Mother! I am asking you and Father a vital question!"

"I know, blessing."

Wendy shuddered. "Please! Don't 'little lamb' me and 'blessing' me, as if I were an offering on the family plate. I am your eldest daughter—and I want to go away and discover myself."

There was a desperate wail to her voice and a deep suspenseful silence. Then with a blinding stab to the eyes, the light leaped on. The drama of the darkness disappeared. Mr. Allardyce no longer resounded as an oracle; he looked the earnest, solemnly humorous, fatherly man that he was—an artist-scientist turned cartographer, who specialized in producing quick but visually accurate maps of world areas for newspapers and magazines; a man who adored daughters and enjoyed his sons—when they all proceeded along the lines of life as he had mapped it.

Mrs. Allardyce, born in Scotland and nourished as a child on folk tales and folk music and the wisdoms of cottage life, became, in the bright light from the chandelier, less the mystic voice of motherly concern and more the practical organizer of family life. Already she was brushing crumbs from the cloth into the palm of her hand.

Rosalyn, the black-haired, and Annetta, the fair, became in the light merely younger sisters—not the chorusing, teasing voices of fate and devilment thrown out in the dark.

And Wendy—there she was, stuck with herself again, illuminated for all to see, with tears on her cheeks and despair in her eyes.

"I'm warning you," she said quietly. "I mean every word about going away."

"Dearest, you're tired," said her mother. "You worked too hard at the end of school. After all, you did take your exams from the infirmary with those infernal tonsils of yours. When you've rested a week or two, you'll feel better about being here. What about the drawings you wanted to make this summer for your friend's story?"

"My friend is spending the summer on the Island of Crete."

"How lucky for her!"

"Very. She's gone alone with her boyfriend."

"Oh."

"Are you shocked? Her parents didn't mind. It meant they didn't have to drive her to the airport."

"I think you're pulling my leg, Wendy."

"Pulling your leg? Oh, you mean putting you on? No. I am not. See? You don't speak as we do. You don't think as we do."

"Oh."

"You can do research for me this summer," Mr. Allardyce announced. "And I can teach you some of the rudiments of map-making."

"I do not want to learn the rudiments of map-making. I only want to research myself."

"I think this discussion has become repetitive." Mr. Allardyce rolled his napkin into his heavy silver ring and placed it emphatically on the table.

"I think it came to a dead end," said Wendy.

Dougal appeared. "There's a very cheerful fire in the

living room. O'Casey is hogging the hearth all by himself."

"Thank you, boys. Girls, let's stack the plates in the pantry. How about a game of Dominoes?"

"By Golly-Gee! This is real Monopoly weather!" exclaimed Mr. Allardyce. "I feel just like a game. Ian, find the box. Annetta, take the cloth off the table. What we all need is a good competitive game!"

"I beg to be excused," said Wendy with caustic politeness and left to join O'Casey by the hearth.

Bright and very early the next morning, before the storm's last traces of damp mist cleared from the tangled branches of the apple-jungle, Wendy quietly left the house. Without a pang of regret she walked past the sign her father had lettered to announce Meridian Farm at the end of the drive.

She carried an old Army rucksack and her lute in its canvas case. Her only regret was the note written in blood and still tucked somewhere under the shingles—that read, "I won't grow up. I swear it by the light of Tinkerbelle and the shadow of Peter Pan."

2

WEARING A RUCKSACK and carrying a lute on a crowded
New York subway was awkward, Wendy found. People
stared at her. She assumed it was because of her brightly
colored cotton shift and her cumbersome impedimenta.
She didn't realize that those who stared at her, seeming
to read her face as if it were another of the advertise-
ment cards spread throughout the train, were drawn by
the freshness of her skin, the clear sparkle of her brown
eyes, and the length of her brown hair, which fell
straight and gleaming halfway to her waist. She
wished she'd tied it back, as the heat in the subway
already could have warmed up a package of frozen
dinner rolls, and it was still early morning.

At home she knew the tide would be high in the
creek, and as soon as the mists cleared and the heat
seeped through, even Rosalyn and Annetta would join
the boys in the Wallow—a bend where they had labori-
ously cut back the tough clods of marsh grass and mud,
digging at the bottom to make a swimming hole. It was
Wendy who had named it the Wallow, because her first
dive off the small plank hopefully placed as a spring-
board had driven her across the width of the bend
and walloped her head onto the opposite bank. She had

emerged, saying, "Proper swimming hole, my neck! All you can do is wallow around and get wet."

"The place is big enough, Wendy!" Dougal insisted. "It's your neck that's too long. Like Alice. Remember the picture of Alice with her long, long neck?"

To her mother's annoyance, Wendy had walked around for weeks afterward with her shoulders bent and her chin pulled down, turtlelike.

"I'm too giraffe!" Wendy explained. "I tower over all the boys in dancing class. It's agony."

Nothing anyone could say could uncrook her, until some of the boys, aged fourteen as she was that year, suddenly shot up to heights respectable for basketball players; her mother brilliantly gave her a pair of pendant silver earrings that winked and gyrated; and a friend of her father, designing a medal on which a Greek goddess appeared, thoughtfully borrowed Wendy to pose because of her classic neck. Thus began her statuesque, classical period which proved more of a bore to her family and friends than her turtle period. As a turtle, she had been pleading and pat-able, eager for a friendly word, humble and self-effacing. But the goddess was aloof, spoke serenely if witheringly, from her height, pierced her ears in a shriekingly bloody midnight scene in a Parsley Hall washroom, and then collected dangling earrings with every cent of money she could scrounge.

Now, in the hot subway car, Wendy clanked the rucksack against her knee and was reassured by the jingle from inside. Her earrings were safely there, and once it was discovered that her whole collection was missing from the painted box on top of her bureau, her family would realize she had indeed left Meridian Farm and her childhood for good.

It had been hard to decide what to take in the rucksack. Even the practice fire drills her father had instigated during their years in the old wooden house, when he blew a whistle in the middle of the night to indicate a sudden fire, hadn't prepared her for the enormity of making a final selection on leaving home. At the blast of the fire-drill whistle, each Allardyce would thump feet on the floor, force open eyelids, grab whatever book lay unfinished by the bed ("I couldn't *bear* not to know how it ended," was always the reason given when Father questioned why a book, a *replaceable* item, was clutched), or whatever battered Teddy or Pooh or Raggedy gave comfort, whatever dress or baseball glove was newest in the closet, whatever merchandised gimmick was the latest status symbol in the gang—from fluorescent Yo-Yo (Ian) to large pink plastic Gooney-Bird (Dougal).

"I despair!" Mr. Allardyce would cry, looking at the indignant sleepy members of his family gathered by the garage—the planned assembly point for an emergency. "Except for your mother, bless her common sense, here you all are again with replaceable commercial items. Especially that depressingly Disneyized pink bird, Dougal."

Mrs. Allardyce yawned and each time displayed the black tin box containing her husband's great-aunt's twin gold bracelets—so small and dainty that no respectable modern female could force her wrists into them—and the black deckled cover of the family photograph album. The children giggled and wondered how long it would take Father to discover that his wife kept those two items on the floor under her side of the double bed, where, in her miserable state of shock because Mr. Allardyce never warned anyone ahead of time about his drills, she could reach down, eyes still unopened, and find at least two irreplaceable items to please him. They had promised each other never to give their mother away because they knew how she suffered at being suddenly wakened—at any hour. The only criticism they ever heard her make about their father was the sleep-tortured cry, "Why does he have to be such a perfectionist about fire drills!"

"Here you all are again with replaceable, commercial items!" Swaying in the heat, Wendy could somehow hear her father's irate voice amid the rattle-clack of the subway rails and the limp rustle of morning newspapers. "I'm disgusted. Have I taught you only to be materialistic? Or do you all have a natural talent for the mundane?"

To which Rosalyn, clutching a new dress she had just made with pain and with pride, replied, "It may be mundane to you, but it's mine-dane to me, and this is the last family fire drill I will ever attend. Don't you think we get enough at Parsley?"

Father, exasperated, replied, "But I only do this to prepare you for an emergency."

Wendy remembered muttering, "We're overrehearsed," and hearing Annetta's final remark, "Why can't we have our own emergencies when we want them?"

She laughed now at her instinct, on packing her rucksack, to include her half-read books. She had! Thoreau's essay on *Civil Disobedience,* Sylvia Ashton-Warner's *Bell Call,* and Henry Roth's *Call It Sleep.* She could replace them at any good paperback bookshop. And her underwear, her bathing suit—all bikini types—took up such a tiny amount of space. She could have stuffed a summer's worth into the outside pockets of the rucksack alone. Her two pairs of blue jeans were neatly wedged in with a silver-conched Navaho belt she treasured and a gold-embroidered scarf of red-silk sari material. "Now that's irreplaceable," she assured herself, "on my allowance."

Perhaps it was her Scots ancestry, instinctively knowledgeable about damps and mists and wind-swept heather on the hills that made her also squeeze in her London Fog raincoat, an Aran Isle sweater, and a long Breton sailor's jersey, useless as they presently seemed.

In the bottom of the bag was the gold watch her father gave her on her sixteenth birthday. She still remembered his sentimental inscription, in his beautiful calligraphy, on the card: "To my firstborn at sweet sixteen," and the sentimental look on his face when he gave it to her. Perfectionist about fire drills and maps, logical yet imaginative in his discussions, he was just plain silly about daughters. His delight in his own spilled over onto their friends to an embarrassing degree. After Parents' Weekends, Wendy had to defend his affectionate ways, even if the defense seemed contradictory. "He's not a dirty old man because he hugs you. He's treating you like a daughter. Unfortunately he adores daughters, and it would be so much easier for us if he didn't! It's a terrible burden for us."

The heaviest weight in the rucksack was all the change—nickels, dimes, and quarters of it. Wendy was materialistic about money. Living on a frugal allowance among some very wealthy girls at Parsley Hall had a definite effect on both Wendy and Rosalyn. They discovered how best to get by on very little cash and talked like snobs in reverse. They didn't buy this, because "everyone had them," or they didn't go there, because "that's where everyone goes." They both hoarded until something really special nagged at them. Wendy's lute, for example, and Rosalyn's wide, handmade silver necklace that she only took off for gym, showers, and posture pictures.

When it came to leaving home that morning, Wendy's only hesitation had been financial. Did she have cash enough to stay away long enough so her family would know how serious she was? It would spoil everything if she had to phone home collect for money! Even with Miggle's family paying the rent and probably most of the food bills, being a girl was expensive. Weekly and monthly necessities always took frightening bites out of her school allowance.

So she decided if she could manage fifty dollars in cash, she could manage eight weeks with Miggle. Miggle dripped money and seldom bothered to count, but she shared better than most girls—she shared, loaned, or gave away everything from Chanel No. 22 to fun-rimmed sunglasses. Wendy had eighteen dollars in cash. She knew where Rosalyn kept her wallet and slipped into her room and rifled it. There was only a disappointing thirteen, which she took and left a note: "I.O.U. $13.00. Your despairing but devoted sister, Wendy." And then, as quietly as possible, she removed Dougal's pink plastic Gooney-Bird, which he carefully lugged to fire drills. Father had somehow never caught on to the slot in the Gooney-Bird's head. It was Dougal's bank.

Eagerly Wendy wrenched the Gooney's head from his threaded neck and spilled the contents onto her bed. But the whole heavy profusion of change only added up to nine dollars and fifty-two cents—still ten dollars short of what she thought she needed. She sat on the bed staring at the coins. Should a whole decision about her future hinge on ten dollars, an arbitrary amount to begin with? *Is Father right? Am I completely materialistic? Where is my sense of adventure? If I give up for lack of a smarmy ten, I'll bow to my parents all my life—Yes, Mother, I'll be in at midnight. No, Father, I won't go out with Wilbur Albee because you don't like him.* All the grinding, teeth-gnashing points of contention in the three weeks since she'd come home from Parsley suddenly churned Wendy's stomach. *They have no right to tell me how to live my life,* she concluded. *So I'll go live it myself.*

She stuck another I.O.U. into the slot in the Gooney-Bird's head, finished packing the rucksack, and exulted in her two-mile freedom march to the train.

She noticed orioles flashing like sun rays through the heavy June leaves in the tall trees. She smelled the salty tang of the hay cut and drying over the marshes toward the sea. The misty dawn floated a pale pinkness through the sky, and she felt as if she were walking through a pearl—all alone. She couldn't see a car or another person, but she felt so joyful that she stopped to wonder about it.

I'm happy because I'm off to be me—uninterfered with, absolutely myself me, she decided. Or was it more unexplainable? Was there really a feeling of happiness that was a rare discovery—that of standing all alone in the world and feeling the ground with its vibrant surging of roots and seeds push strongly under her feet and the thrust of her body up into air, into space—of feeling completely a part of the universe? Was that joy?

From far away came the harsh squawk of the diesel-train's horn. She could see three small cars worming along the track. Wendy scrambled through a wooded shortcut, down a slope, running to meet the train as if all the bad dreams of her childhood were chasing her.

Her mental review of her early morning escape came to a sudden shuddering stop, as her subway train arrived at a station. Wendy ducked to stare out the train window at the station name. It was the one nearest Miggle's.

As she hurried toward the door, a man's heel came down hard on her bare sandaled toes, and she screeched, scaring the man. He stared at her boldly, apparently deciding that any nut who didn't wear shoes on the subway deserved to be stepped on, then shrugged at her, and turned away.

Wendy limped up the stairs, suddenly conscious of the dirt and the filthy papers caught into corners, the spit globbed here and there. Her bare toes curled inward, until she resolutely stopped looking at the ground.

Four blocks away toward the East River was Miggle's apartment building, towering and glassy. People were just now hurrying away from this residential area to jobs in stores and offices, or taking their dogs for a morning curbing. Wendy found herself greeting each face with an eager look, though what she was looking for she didn't know. Some sign of welcome to her new life, perhaps. Or some acknowledgment of fellow existence. But most faces were shut, preoccupied—already at work or still home in bed. She did rate one or two amused smiles. *If I were lugging a bass viol, I might even get a laugh,* she decided.

She rated a very hard stare from the doorman at Miggle's building, as she started to walk under the deep blue and gold awning to the revolving door. She stared back at him solemnly, tired of giving away a smile with no return. She'd seen that speculative look before, in shops where Miggle spent while Wendy watched or restaurants where the headwaiter, after a brief glance, quickly saw a table and unhooked his plush rope to let them through. *He's running me through his status computer,* Wendy knew, *to see if I belong here. The long hair and the earrings are it, but he's not sure about the feet. But he sees my feet are clean and so is my neck.* She couldn't help tossing her hair. *The lute case is doubtful. Shall I explain it is not a guitar? He'd stop me sure if I had on my blue jeans, but he's given up trying to classify dresses. It's the rucksack that's got him!*

Wendy laughed, and the man took a quick step toward her, scowling. "Just a minute, miss. You'll have to tell me whom you want to see."

"Miss Margaret Louise Banbury. In Twelve-C."

His eyebrows stopped rising. "I believe the Banburys have left."

"Maybe her parents. But she's expecting me."

"I'll see."

He stepped to his telephone, framed like an *objet d'art* in its stone niche. "Your name?"

"Miss Allardyce."

The man had perfected a way of inserting his voice into the phone while barely moving his lips. He could be saying anything about her—that she was a peddler or an anarchist. How silly it all was, to be computerized, sized up, and announced or unannounced, according to one person's views. But at least he'd roused someone to the phone.

"You may go up, miss."

Wendy stopped herself from saying, "Thank you kindly, sir." He took his job so seriously, she had a feeling it would be lost on him.

But he didn't twirl the door for her, and it was a tight fit with the rucksack and the lute case.

The elevators were self-service, which she hated, and the ride was ghostly silent and swift. She was relieved when the doors parted at last to reveal the hushed and carpeted corridor. Miggle often yodeled in the hall. "Just trying to make myself heard. You could die out here in this stillness, and no one would ever know till he stepped on you and felt bones on the carpet." Wendy walked quickly and jabbed the pearl door button at 12-C.

She had just swung her rucksack off her back, when the door opened. Instead of Miggle, there stood her older brother Peter.

His longish black hair, uncombed, looked like a fright wig and his beard was still in a state of being coaxed. Wendy noticed that he had better luck growing hair on his chest than his chin. He was obviously only half awake and had pulled on the first pair of pants handy when the doorbell rang. He looked at her without enchantment.

"Come in." He yawned wrenchingly, stretching from top to bottom, walked through the foyer into the living room, sagged onto a couch, and stared at her. "What do you want so very early in the morning?"

Wendy put down the lute and the rucksack. "Miggle. Is she still asleep?"

"Maybe. I wouldn't know."

"Well—I won't bother you. I'll just wait here until she gets up."

"You'll have a long wait, because you won't know when she gets up."

"What do you mean?"

"She's not here. So you won't know when she gets up."

"Oh! When is she coming back?"

"About the middle of August."

"The middle of August! Where is she? When did she go?"

"She's in Ireland. Flew over yesterday. There's some girl at her school—that's where I've seen you before—at Miggle's school! I knew I knew you from somewhere! Anyway, there's some girl whose father is a movie director and has a place in Ireland, and she called up three days ago and asked Miggle to stay with her."

"I know the one. Duffy. I thought Miggle didn't like her much."

"I don't know. She was lonely and she called up from Ireland and Miggle felt sorry for her and off she went. But she'll probably get bored and be back by the middle of July. What did you want her for?"

"It seems that Miggle forgot something."

"What?"

"Me. She asked me to come and spend the summer with her so she could stay here in New York. In this apartment."

"Did she now!" said Peter, putting on an Irish brogue. "The impudence of the spalpeen. Invitin' yer and leavin' yer, all a' twonce. Well, tell me your name so I'll know to whom I'm speaking—and you've got a choice of bedrooms—daft Miggle's, my mother's mirrored lair, my father's room, although it looks like a locker room and you might trip over the rowing machine in the dark. Or mine, if you're not fussy about either the dust or me. I'm not."

It all fell out of his lips like a line of chat he wasn't even listening to and Wendy sighed. She felt suddenly hot and tired and quite thirsty. She hadn't made herself any breakfast at home because her father could hear the footsteps of a mouse in a kitchen cupboard and take the scrabble for an invitation to early eggs and bacon.

But however much she determined to leave home, now without Miggle's help, she could hardly spend the summer in 12-C with Miggle's brother.

She stood up, suddenly furious. "If Miggle should ring you up from Dumochree or Ballyfoggle or whatever place she is, just tell her Wendy Allardyce, her dear friend who just had an all-out fight with her parents over coming to New York to keep Miggle company for the summer, did come—and she has left."

3

"Not so fast!" said Peter, suddenly coming wide-awake and trying to study Wendy unobtrusively, but she felt his attitude change like a brisk shift in the wind. "You've brought luggage. You're here. You've got all summer, if you've had a fight with your parents. I suggest we make some coffee, and you tell me all about it. *Wendy Allardyce.* Now I remember—you were Wendy in the school play. My parents made me go because Miggle was Nana, although you sure couldn't recognize her in that dog suit."

"That was a whole year ago, and I've been trying to live it down ever since. I should take some chalk and go around writing graffiti like 'Tinkerbelle is Turned Off' or 'Never-Never Land is a Bad Trip.' Anything to get it out of my system."

"Now that's interesting. Has your shrink suggested you act out your aggressions?"

"I don't need a shrink, thank you."

"You don't have to be defensive about it. Some people do and some people don't. Live and let live, you know. Do you know how to make coffee?"

"If it's instant."

"It is."

From the foyer a round, carpeted stairwell led to the floor below, where a massive dining table surrounded by twelve chairs seemed to be waiting in solemnity for a board meeting. Long chalk-white drapes covered the windows, and three tremendous paintings almost covered each of the chalk-white walls. One was done in raw streaks of color, the others in monochromatic shapes and overlaps of tones. Wendy stopped to gape.

"My mother considers herself a connoisseur of contemporary art. She is very proud of one Pethko and two Daubs. I eat with my eyes shut."

Peter shoved through the swinging door to the efficient kitchen, where the white-porcelain cupboards gleamed like a row of capped teeth. Chrome appliances waited to come alive at a touch and whirr and champ at their job. Wendy giggled nervously.

"What's the matter?" Peter found the teakettle and filled it.

"This kitchen is so—uncomfortable," Wendy decided, thinking of the wood-paneled room at home which had an old brick wall with warming ovens, iron crane and kettle, and huge firedogs inside the fireplace; rocking chairs, a pine dry sink bright with geraniums in winter, and a large battered table with great yellow crockery bowls standing on it for bread dough or tremendous summer garden salads. "This is ridiculous. I expect the refrigerator to open its mouth like a hungry mechanical hippopotamus and the oven to sound off with the taped roar of a caged lion."

"You are a very imaginative girl. I never saw anything here beyond a scientific laboratory. I used to hope for Dr. Jekyll and Mr. Hyde. But all we had was Myrtle and then May-Evelyn—now on her vacation. Myrtle didn't stay very long. I guess she felt the same way I do about this place. She used to start reciting a poem, only she couldn't remember the ending. If I ever hear the ending, I'm supposed to send it to her. But it's not likely. It was part of Myrtle's youth—not mine."

"How did it go?"

Oh—the Antiseptic Baby and the Prophylactic Pup
Were playing in the Garden when the Bunny
    gamboled up.

"It's not naughty. It's just totally sterile."

"Let's take the coffee upstairs." Wendy had the shivers from the atmosphere, and Peter's bare chest looked goosepimply.

"I must have given the air-conditioning an extra twist when I came in last night. Here's a tray."

They found cups, the instant coffee, cream, butter, and a package of cold cuts, some cheese, and some rye bread.

"My favorite breakfast!" said Wendy.

"That's hopeful. So far, I think we'll get along very well." Peter said it in such a matter-of-fact voice that she didn't think about it. He put the tray down in the middle of the living-room rug—fluffy beige wool from Greece. They sat cross-legged, and since Wendy couldn't think of anything to say and she was starving, she ate.

Peter ate, too, but occasionally he gave her a swift appraising look. After his second cup of coffee, he said, "I've come to the conclusion, thankfully, that you are not at all like my sister."

"Miggle is a very expansive, out-going person."

"You're being polite. Miggle is bossy, nosy, and noisy. Shallow, selfish, and silly."

"You don't know her very well. She isn't shallow and she's not selfish. She's very generous with all kinds of things. And she did invite me for the summer—"

"And promptly social-climbed to Ireland, to be with a movie-director's daughter. What are you—dumb? or humble? I'd kick you out now if I thought you were either."

"It isn't your choice as to whether I go or stay," said

Wendy with indignation. "It's mine. Thank you very much, but of course I'm not going to stay."

"Why not?"

"Look—my parents weren't even going to let me stay here with your *sister*. That's what the argument was about. It's so stupid. I'm old enough to do what I want when I want to."

"Are you?"

"Of course. I was seventeen last month."

"Age has nothing to do with it. My guess is that your parents are right. You really are Wendy Darling, all innocence and purity, and if Peter Pan came and said he'd teach you how to fly to Never-Never Land, you'd go and mother the boys. You'd bake cakes and mend pockets and tell bedtime stories. But in the end you'd be longing to fly home, because you'd know Mr. and Mrs. Darling and Nana were all forlorn and waiting for you."

Wendy felt a fury of confusion and contradiction rising inside her. She was insulted that Peter Banbury would put her down so, considering her a little girl—all innocence and country and wide-eyed. But, whether she liked it or not, that's what she was, and she was equally furious because she'd given it away. *If only I didn't have a face as obvious as a traffic light,* she mourned. *Everyone can see the stop-and-go thoughts flashing on and off behind it.*

"So I really bugged you?" asked Peter, but sympathetically. "I'll bet it's this way: you're a terribly nice girl. But you just can't stand it at home now because you're up-tight about your parents. So you walked out. But you expected Miggle to be here, and camping out in a duplex apartment in New York with a school chum could be quite a thing, couldn't it? You'd show Mater and Pater they couldn't run your life, but it would be a safe place and you wouldn't starve. Right?"

"You really do bug me. You're so—smarmy."

"*Smarmy!* What kind of a word is that? Something right out of *Little Women?*"

"Now I remember why Miggle told me she couldn't stand you. You have a superiority complex."

"What old-fashioned terminology! Psychology as taught at Parsley must be from ancient texts. I do not have a superiority complex. I have strong ego needs which I express aggressively to reinforce my creativity quotient."

"Wow. With a small 'W.'"

Peter laughed. "Look—let's not fight. You're in a spot. You don't know either what you ought to do or what you want to do. Right?"

"Yes. You're right," Wendy admitted.

"I'm five years older than you and vastly more experienced at in-fighting with parents, at survival in the hungry world, well—at everything. You name it. I've tried it. But tell me about you. As they say, rapping helps."

"You've figured most of it out. Actually what bothers me is that my parents gave us a happy, secure, and kind of imaginative childhood. I should be grateful. There's been a frightening amount of love and attention poured into it. But right now it's smothering me. It's too much togetherness. Daddy's omnipresent. He wants to know everything I do and everywhere I go. Maybe it isn't nosiness so much as just not wanting to be left out of things. My mother wants to know the insides of all my friends—what they think, what they hope. It's embarrassing. They sit there in the kitchen, beaming and smiling and inviting everyone for cookies and games. As if we were babies."

"Tough. There are kids who would envy you."

"I know. That's why I'm ashamed and I feel guilty. And I don't want to. I want to be free and be happy about it."

"I know a real hip shrink. If you feel guilty, you need one."

"Oh, stop it! I ought to be able to work things out for myself. I do know I'm not going to go home. And I'm not going to stay here."

"All right. We know why you're not going home. Give me the reasons why you aren't going to stay here. If you're out to jolt your parents, shacking up in an apartment for the summer with a twenty-two-year-old male acquaintance is a pretty good start at defiance. Maybe you don't like me. Or you don't trust me."

"In the first place, my family may be on the phone any minute. Then my father would be on the doorstep and drag me away in humiliation. And you're wrong. I don't—not like you. I don't even know you. You don't sound at all like any boy I've ever known, either."

"Callow youth. No competition."

"I'm not sure I'd trust you, though—in some ways."

"That's a point for discussion. How much do I trust thee? Let me count the ways."

"Be serious. This is a serious discussion." Wendy stared at the tufts of wool on the rug, tugging at one. "I just don't think staying here would solve anything."

"Ah-ha! At last you've come out with a good reason. Why wouldn't it solve anything?"

"For the reasons you said. It's safe and I wouldn't starve—as long as you can cook. But it would just be transferring from one cocoon to another."

"And you must burst out of your cocoon this summer? Your wings are stirring?"

"They're stirring."

"To the point where you want some action?"

"Yes. I've got myself all psyched up, and so I have to find the action."

Peter was silent a moment or two. He looked at her, starting to suggest something, hesitated, and finally decided to go ahead. He scrunched around on the carpet and leaned forward earnestly. "What will you do when you leave here?"

Wendy was surprised to find it was the getting away,

not the staying away, that had been her only concern. She suddenly realized she hadn't thought much about what she and Miggle would do with their time, although they'd talked about exploring the Village. There was a girl from school who had sworn she was going to spend the summer there. With her long red hair and her nickname of 'Arriet, she shouldn't be hard to find.

"I think," Wendy decided as she spoke, "I'll go to the Village. I may be able to find someone I know there."

"You're sure that's what you want to do?" Peter asked. "All of your own accord?"

"All of my own accord," Wendy repeated. Then she laughed as she remembered an A.A. Milne poem her mother used to read to them.

> Last seen wandering vaguely
> Quite of her own accord
> She went down to the end of the town
> Forty shillings reward.

"Yes. Definitely. I shall go down to the end of the town and never mind the reward."

"Since you're that committed to looking for the action, how about taking a trip with me?"

Her reaction was silent surprise. So he went on. "There you are with that innocent fasten-your-seat-belt sign on your face again. How are you going to break away from all your old concepts if you react like the heroine in a melodrama? 'Oh, help, help! Save me!' You're trying to convince yourself you don't want to be saved. Right?"

Wendy nodded. She felt numb, as if this unexpected conversation were taking place between Peter Banbury and some girl she'd just met. "Trip has a lot of meanings. Which do you mean? A journey trip? Or an acid trip?"

As soon as she asked that, she felt Peter react like a car, shifting up from low gear and settling satisfactorily into a smooth speedy glide.

"Actually I meant a trip trip. You know—a voyage of discovery."

"Getting stoned is supposed to do that. Take you on a voyage of discovery."

"Sure. Except that it's all inside yourself. I'm just suggesting join Peter Banbury and see some of the world."

"Join Peter Pan and see Never-Never Land?" Wendy pulled and pulled at a twist of wool in the rug.

"It's up to you to make out of it whatever you put into it. Anyway, you have till noontime to make up your mind. I'm leaving then."

"Now you tell me. What about tickets and passports and money?"

"You do have a literal mind. Where do you think we're going? Istanbul? Katmandu? You don't need a passport—yet—to the lower East side."

Wendy sat up, excited. "You do mean the Village and around there."

"Thereabouts. Is the Village the Great-Big-Electric-Acid-Cooled Mecca to you?"

"I don't know. I've been through it now and then."

"Going through it and staying in it are two different things. I'm not coming back here, you know. If you go with me, you'll have to take whatever goes on. It won't be a Parcheesi game with apartment Twelve-C on Seventy-second Street as Home Safe. I wonder if you're brave enough."

"Honestly!" Wendy exploded. "It's not darkest Africa or the first lunar landing. It's New York City."

"Partly correct. Mostly it's people."

"Why are you going?"

"To renew some friendships. To see what a difference a year makes—in myself and my friends. Besides, I can't stand one more day of being a cog in a Wall-Street office machine for my father's sake. He got me a summer job in a brokerage house. I told him as soon as he left on his trip and quit escorting me there personally every morning, I'd quit. He said if I quit, I could quit living here. So I'm just living up to my side of the bargain. If he doesn't like it, you know where he can shove it."

"Do you know the Village?"

"I've lived there."

"When?"

"Last summer. My parents thought I spent ten weeks in Montreal working at Expo. Ha! I was sixty blocks from home. In another country."

"Are you a tripper? An acid-head?"

"I've been the route," Peter said flatly. "Why do you think I'm going back?"

Wendy was uneasy. She was acutely aware that talking about doing something felt abstract. But when it came to picking up her lute and her rucksack and walking out of 12-C with Peter Banbury, her feelings would be very real.

So far she hadn't burned any bridges. She could still go back home tonight with some dumb excuse like having taken her lute to be repaired in New York.

Peter stood up. "I'm not urging you to come. I could get into trouble that way too easy. I'm just saying you can tag along if you like. You can stay with me, or you can go off on your own. Or you can run home to the nursery any time. Well?"

"I'm thinking."

"If you have to think about it, you can't be very committed to discovering yourself."

"That's a nasty crack. Can't I think about how and where I want to discover myself?"

"Sure. Figure out your options. Just let me know in half an hour."

"I'll wash up the coffee things." Wendy put the debris of their breakfast on the tray. Peter started for his bedroom when the phone rang. He stopped in the foyer to answer it.

"This is Peter Banbury speaking. No, my sister isn't here. She's away for the summer. . . . My parents are, too. Sorry, I didn't catch your name. Mr. Allardyce? Oh, how do you do, sir."

Wendy quickly placed the tray on the white-marble coffee table. Her hands were shaking too much to hold it. Her stomach tightened into a knot, and she shivered with tenseness.

"Well, to be honest, sir, I do know Wendy. But why did you think she would be coming here?"

Wendy flapped her arms frantically. "Don't tell him I'm here!" she mouthed.

Peter pointed urgently at the front door. Wendy walked quickly to the door, and went out, closing it firmly behind her, much as she wanted to eavesdrop. Her family certainly hadn't wasted any time checking up on her! Still treating her like a five-year-old! She stood there, shaking, in the hallway. The dimness, the thick carpet, the quiet made her feel as if she were isolated in a padded cell. No wonder Miggle had to yell now and then in the hall.

She alternated between being furious with her father and frightened at the suddenness with which she'd walked out of his range, away from his protective custody—and into what? Then she grew furious at herself for feeling frightened. Where was the girl who had stood bravely in the dark by the family dinner table proclaiming her independence? Where was the girl who had exulted over her freedom, her oneness with the world, in the pearly dawn? Was she just a chicken-child after all?

The door opened. Peter looked at her soberly. "You made your decision. You walked out."

"I guess it was instinctive. Like your parents tell you to do something, so you do the opposite."

"Maybe. Anyway, I could honestly tell your father you'd been here, and you'd gone, and you hadn't told me where you were going. I said for all I knew you'd be home tonight, since you found Miggle wasn't here."

"Did he buy that? My coming home?"

"It's what he hopes. But he seemed to think because you'd taken all your earrings you weren't going to rush home. What's the big significance about your earrings?"

"They're my collection. My prize possession except for my lute."

"I see. That reminds me—what *things* shall I take with me? It's wise to have wampum to trade with natives. Beads and flowers and old uniforms. Watches and transistor radios and gold cigarette lighters?"

She followed his glance around the living room—at rare objects placed to catch the eye: a large Steuben vase, a bronze Javanese bust, an ivory fan, a Chinese screen. "Things, things, things—which things shall I choose?"

But he wandered into his bedroom and started throwing clothes into a cheap zippered bag. "Too bad I lost my Boy Scout knapsack."

"You never were one!" Wendy protested. "How can they have Boy Scouts in the city?"

"You are a country chick. An ignorant, bucolic bird. First you knock shrinks and now Boy Scouts. We met in church basements, you boob. Just like half the Boy Scouts in the country probably do."

Wendy again picked up the tray. She washed up the things in the desolate kitchen and put them away, but she stuck the rest of the cheese in the pocket of her dress. When she came back up the stairwell, Peter was talking on the phone.

"Mr. Means? Peter Banbury. I hope my not getting in this morning hasn't inconvenienced you, sir. That's good. I rather suspected it was a job you made up at my father's request. Yes, I saw them off yesterday. I called to tell you that you won't have to worry about finding things for me to do. I'm resigning. Well, it was long enough to see what astute men you have to be—and I know I'm not cut out for that kind of brainwork. Yes, I did tell my father. Yes, he gave me his considered opinion, too. At length. Oh, I have something else to do. I'll be busy—don't you worry. Thank you, sir. Have a good summer."

Wendy decided to change to her blue jeans. She took her rucksack into Miggle's room. Before she closed the door, she heard Peter dial again. "It's all set," she heard him say softly. "Better than we could ever have planned. By sheer luck I've stumbled onto the absolutely perfect girl. So I won't have to find one. She'll be great. What? No, you'd better believe it. She's an absolutely innocent bird."

4

WENDY SAT on Miggle's bed, staring out the window at the windows glaring back at her from across the street. What kind of a fellow was Peter Banbury anyway?

Here he was, going off on his own in protest against a job he disliked. But there was something else underneath. He sounded like two different people on the phone—first, the smooth, secure, bored young man politely addressing a friend of his father's; and then a rather excited guy planning something with someone else.

Planning what? And why did she fit perfectly into this unknown scheme? Because she was an absolutely innocent bird, who unwittingly fitted his purpose. The words "Peter Banbury has plans for an innocent bird" began to rock around in her head to the tune of *Eleanor Rigby*.

Two things maddened Wendy. One was discovering that someone thought she was dumb, stupid, or innocent. The words seemed interchangeable to her at the moment. The other was finding that someone was using her. Annetta was very clever at using Wendy, because she was a subtle needler. More than once Wendy had fought for some privilege at home only to find that

Annetta was the one who benefited most from it and realized later it was her youngest sister who had made her sow the seed of discontent.

Wendy had woken up halfway through the year at school and discovered she continually fetched and carried for her roommate. But when Wendy confronted her about it, Linda Lou told her without even a blink that she was going to room with another girl next year, a real charmin' girl full of sincere character. Wendy spent the rest of the year being full of sincere character and extremely prickly.

She could be prickly to Peter Banbury, too. The impression he gave of complete confidence annoyed her. He was definitely the kind who needed to be shot down. What better way to do it than pretend to go along with his scheme—and then spoil it? It would certainly fit in with her needs far more than lugging her lute and earrings back on the next train to Westerly.

He knocked on the door. "Have you decided where you're going? I'm about to leave."

"Just a minute." She fastened the Navaho belt over her low-slung jeans and folded the dress. The cheese fell out of the pocket, and she threw it into the knapsack along with her clothes. She checked her wallet again and stuffed it as far into the bottom of the pack as she could. She kept several dollars in the pocket of her jeans. The Breton sailor's jersey with its long sleeves was too big for her, but she liked its loose comfort. Remembering how hot it was on the subway, she tied back her hair with a scarf from Miggle's closet.

Peter was checking windows, like any responsible householder. Wendy realized that he seemed to talk in one way, but act in another. She couldn't figure him out.

"Blast! This curtain thing must be stuck." Peter climbed onto the wide shelf beneath the windows, a shelf that topped cabinets built wall to wall and hid the life-support systems that kept apartment dwellers comfortable in their capsules—the air-conditioner, the humidifier, the heating units, the stereo speakers, the minimal space for storage of the few artifacts kept by atticless families.

He struggled to free whatever boggle kept the silver-brocade curtains from opening and closing on their track at the touch of a switch. Then he turned to leap down.

"Oh, no!" laughed Wendy, but it was a rather high-pitched artificial laugh, as unreal as the whole situation suddenly seemed to her.

"What's so funny?"

"It haunts me—the whole Peter Pan bit. Look at you—standing up there against the window. I should gaze past you and see the deep-blue sky of the backdrop and a dozen gold stars winking on and off as the stage crew works the light board. And the orchestra tunes up, and you surreptitiously check your harness, and then you sail across the room at me, aiming for the mantelpiece and flashing your teeth madly and singing 'I'm Fly-ing—'"

"Who do you think I am? Mary Martin?"

"'I'm Flying,'" sang Wendy.

"You'll never get off the ground. You don't think lovely thoughts."

"Candy!" sang Wendy. "Presents! Christmas!" She leaped around the room, arms outstretched, hair bouncing, singing at the top of her lungs. Let Peter Banbury think she was a kook. That should convince him she hadn't a brain to use on any counterscheme of her own.

"Hey, hey," said Peter rather disgustedly, still standing above it all on his perch. "I saw that TV program, too. Umpty times. But don't try flying without wires—"

"Who needs wires?" Wendy backed off and went at the overstuffed couch full tilt, intending to use her best ballet *tour jeté* and leap over it. But her foot hit the top, and like a disappointed high jumper, she flipped and landed on her back on the rug. How humiliating! It was like the lights going off in the middle of her scene at home. Some girls would have gone over like a gazelle —and probably ended up with a career in the theater, dancing with Edward Villella. But not Wendy Allardyce.

She lay on the rug, getting her breath back. Peter's face loomed over her. How funny it was to look up at a bearded chin from below. It wiggled so foolishly when he spoke. "Are you sure you aren't putting me on? Aren't you already on a trip?"

"Who, me? What do you think I am, stoned?" She sat up. "The only stones I see out in the country where I live are real solid rocks."

"I'm not so sure about that. I'm not so sure that you're for real."

"Well, I've decided. I'll give you a chance to find out. I'm going with you."

He hesitated. She really had him puzzled now—just as he puzzled her. Then he reached out and pulled her up.

"Come along, then. Only we'd better not be seen leaving together. You know—in case your father starts up a search party. You don't want the doorman to be able to say you left with me. Between my driver's license, my draft card, my social security number and my ID-card, my Gulf Oil card, and the numbers the laundry stamps in my shirts, I'm too easy to find somewhere."

Wendy wondered if that was his real reason for suggesting they leave separately, but he did have a point. "Shall I go first?"

"Sure. Meet me in Washington Square—near the arch —in an hour."

She picked up her lute and the rucksack. He held the door for her politely. "In case I'm late, don't go away. I'll get there," he promised. "I'm going to see if I can locate a guy. It might make a difference in where we go tonight."

"Oh?"

"Sure. Wouldn't you rather live with the Lost Boys or Tiger Lily than the Pirates?"

"Look! I'm stuck with the name Wendy and having been in that foolish play. You are stuck with the name Peter—"

"I'm not stuck with it. I like it."

"That's not the point. I'm sick of this Peter Pan business. Not just the symbolic not-growing-up stuff. But the whole circumstance! It's not my bag. So don't keep bringing it up!"

"I'm not the one who went flapping about the room and tried to fly over a couch."

"I know. I get hysterical now and then. But let's just forget J. M. Barrie and all his little—characters."

"I agree. I certainly don't care for a kooky boy's part that has always been played by skinny women without beards. I'll see you in an hour."

The elevator sank silently to the lobby. The insulation of coolness and quietness which made her decision seem remote and unreal upstairs was shattered as soon as she stepped out on the sidewalk. The noonday sun and noon-traffic noise blasted her. The doorman, tortured in the heat of his uniform, leaned against the building, looking as if he yearned for stone to turn to ice.

Wendy reached Washington Square long before the hour was up. She bought an ice-cream sandwich from a vendor and stood around, watching people in the dusty park. How small and caged the trees seemed, weighted down by their leaves in the heat, and how drab were the birds. Brown sparrows, hopping and fighting, and gray pigeons fussing about, looking too awkward to fly. It seemed as though the orioles flashing through the towering trees that morning were part of another life. *Well, that's what you wanted,* said Wendy to herself. *You're here. Go ahead. Enjoy it.*

She sat on a bench, rucksack and lute beside her—and watched, without feeling part of the scene at all. Perhaps it was the heat and the intense light that made it seem lifeless, or as if someone had stopped the action in a movie. People flopped on benches and the grass, like fish gasping stiffly out of water. Mothers used strident voices to jerk children back when they wandered away. Dogs dragged their owners at the end of a leash. On one patch of tattered grass a boy, naked above his waist except for the long hair splayed across his shoulders and the ropes of beads across his chest, played his guitar and sang. But he played a routine accompaniment with no style, and he sang poorly. Except for the girl next to him wearing a man's T-shirt and jeans and holding the boy's T-shirt in case the police tried to throw him out of the park for either singing at the wrong time without a permit or not wearing a shirt in public, no one paid any attention to him. *Why can't people who feel compelled to sing in public at least do it well?* Wendy wondered. This boy whined, but without the intensity of Bob Dylan.

An old man, whose clothes smelled as if they'd been sewn onto him for months, sat down. She quickly slid the strap of her rucksack over her arm and hooked her fingers through her lute-case handle. "You got a guitar?" the man asked. "Play me a tune. I don't want nothin' but you play me a tune."

"It's not a guitar," Wendy said quickly and turned her back on him.

"Jest asked a question," muttered the man and sat there, rubbing his hands over the bench until his fingers squawked out a noise like chalk shrieking on a blackboard. It was a sound that always set Wendy's teeth on edge. She jumped up and walked slowly around the square.

After her third circuit of the park, the bottoms of her feet stung and burned against the hard leather soles of her sandals. She could feel the city grit between her toes. The old man who'd asked for a tune had fallen asleep, sprawled like a spilled trash can over the bench. So she sat down opposite, thankful to be off her feet.

She began to feel very important. What was Peter arranging that could take so long? What was there to arrange in Village life anyway? You met some people and shared their scene and stayed in their pad, and then you met some other people and moved to their pad. That was the freedom. No reservations. No hotel register. No introductions. No real names, perhaps. Just friends. Real people. It had to be that way, because that was the point of it all. She felt quite safe in her expectations that this was the way it would be, because that was the mystique reported right from Haight-Ashbury, or from the Village itself. She'd heard it and read it, so she knew it was true.

It was the heat that was numbing her. She felt the cloth of her jeans pull away from the hot, green bench slats as she stood up and stretched. Her outflung hand struck someone behind her. It was Peter.

"Are you sure you're not a secret student of karate?"

"Do you always sneak up on people?"

"I thought you were asleep, and I didn't want to scare you."

"I almost was," Wendy laughed at herself. "How's that for an anticlimax? I renounce home and mother and hot baths and accomplish nothing more than a surreptitious snooze in Washington Square. Well, are we off?"

"We are."

She picked up her things and turned in the direction of the Village.

"That's not the way I'm going," Peter announced. "Here. Let me carry your rucksack and you carry your guitar."

"It's not a guitar. It's a lute."

"Zounds! That's right. You did mention it. You really grow on a guy. Why the lute?"

"Because everyone else has a guitar. Because I adore

Julian Bream. I wish I could have brought his records. Peter, you didn't bring very much!"

Peter carried a medium-sized beat-up zipper-closed bag. He wore dark glasses, a long-sleeved open-necked shirt of rough blue material. *Some kind of peasant shirt,* Wendy decided, and wished she had one like it. He had on well-worn blue jeans with a rope belt and sandals. Around his neck was a chain and a rather awkwardly thick silver pendant with an embossed design on it. That surprised Wendy, but she wasn't sure why. Perhaps it was because she felt Peter Banbury was more artistic and had better taste than to wear such a poorly designed object. But maybe medallions were meant to be symbols, not works of art. He fingered it thoughtfully, as he told her to follow him. Perhaps it was so heavy he didn't like it to swing and bang against his chest.

"Ready? Off to see the world with Peter Banbury? Via yellow submarine or hot-air balloon or ocean-going tug?"

Wendy's face tilted eagerly up at Peter, delight in her adventure suddenly returning as imagination buoyed her up. "I'm ready."

"Then there's nothing like a down-to-earth beginning. Back to the subway."

"But I thought you were going to stay in the Village."

"If you're going to stick with me, learn one thing fast. Be flexible. You know the biggest problem with people? It isn't just conformity. It's flexibility. That stuff about 'I can't go because I always do something else at this moment.' Half of life gets unlived that way."

"So I'm getting the deluxe guided tour. With lectures."

"Right. And now, miss, just step this way. Right down to the bowels of New York and on to Grand Central."

"Whatever for?"

"Because we're going to Boston."

"Boston!"

"Do you know you have a very annoying habit? You repeat what I just said. Yes, Boston."

"But why? What's Boston got to offer?"

"That's where it's at now. Boston Common. Everyone's headed there. You don't want to miss out on the big scene, do you?"

"No. I guess I just hadn't thought any farther than being right in New York."

"In apartment Twelve-C. You see? You're not being flexible."

"Oh, yes, I am. I'm going with you."

The atmosphere in Grand Central was breathless, as if all the breathable air had risen up into the heights of the ceiling and the leftover air below hardly had enough oxygen to keep people moving.

Peter walked steadily toward the track posting the train to Boston. Wendy sighed. It was not a limited. It stopped everywhere, including Westerly. She hoped no one on the train would know her. "Peter—you forgot to get tickets."

"Have them already."

"Two?"

"Two."

"You were awfully sure I'd come."

"I felt irresistible. Hurry up. The train's about to go."

They hauled themselves into the last car, and Peter headed for the double seats at the end of the section. Luckily they were unoccupied, as the train wasn't crowded. He lifted the lute and the rucksack onto the rack and left his zipper bag on the empty seat facing them. Wendy sat by the dirt-streaked window.

In a few minutes the train started off, protesting with every jolt. Peter put his head back and closed his eyes. There Wendy sat, surprised at how this day had turned out after all and surprised at herself, wondering what she would do when the train stopped at Westerly. Should she stay with this crazy caper? Or turn coward and sneak off toward home?

Suddenly they came up out of the tunnel and into the harsh afternoon view of city windows. Wendy felt literally beside herself. There she was, Wendy Allardyce, slumped in the heat on a sticky train, a stranger at the moment even to herself, going somewhere, even if she wasn't sure why. She was a person doing her own thing all right—but what was it? Part of her felt alive and aware, uneasy, almost ready to push the panic button. But the rest of her sat there with an open mind like a video tape, recording faces at city windows, messages on great billboards, snatches of life below in discarded yards and unknown streets—recording it all on her mind whether she needed it there or not because, she supposed, that's what this trip was all about.

5

AS THE CONDUCTOR came along, Wendy suddenly turned her back on Peter and stared out the window.

"Are you pretending you're not with me?" Peter muttered in her ear. "What's the matter?"

"It's the same man who was on the train this morning. He might recognize me and remember I got on at Westerly. I don't really dare look around too much in case there's anyone I know."

Peter studied her face. "With your hair tied back and that makeup job on your eyes, you don't even look like the same girl who came to find Miggle."

"That's good." Wendy relaxed. "Maybe that's why I enjoy being in plays. With makeup and costumes you can feel absolutely like someone else. It's a tremendous relief."

"Don't you like being yourself?"

Wendy stared at Peter in surprise. "That's an awfully personal question. Do you always want to turn people's feelings inside out and poke at them when you've only just met?"

"Is it a question you don't want to think about?" he countered.

That forced Wendy to think about it. Peter idly

reached for his zipper bag, unzipped the top, fished about until he found a pack of cigarettes, started to take them out, and remembered they were in the No Smoking section. "Bletch!" he said and stuck the bag between them on the seat. "No smoking."

"Don't mind me. Go find the Smoking Car."

"No. I'd rather have your company than the company of a cigarette."

"You'd never get a job in an advertising company with a nonslogan like that!"

"I'd never want one. Advertising is the real Never-Never Land. Phony people. Phony values, even phony words."

"If you don't like phony words, why do you say things like 'Zounds' and 'Bletch?' "

"Don't they sound better than the usual run of unimaginative expletives and overworked oaths? Most people are terribly dull when they swear. But you didn't answer my question. Do you like being in plays because you don't like being yourself?"

"I don't know. I never thought about it that way. At school you have to do something, and if you hate field hockey and volley ball as much as I do, you go out for chorus or dance or theater. I liked theater the most. And then we always used to dress up and make up plays at home."

"Tell me about home."

"Why?"

"Because I'm interested. You had an argument with your parents—and you split. One disagreement doesn't usually produce such a step. So I'm curious. What are your parents like? Your brothers and sisters? What kind of homelife do you have?"

"Are you writing a book or practicing to be a shrink?" Wendy and her friends liked to spend hours talking about themselves, but the excitement was in the telling, not the listening. She was suspicious of anyone who asked questions and volunteered to listen.

Peter continued to look her right in the eye, although he did grin. "There's a lot more to you than to many of the many girls I've met. And I've met just about every kind. Real hippie, plastic hippie, serious career girl, career girl serious about finding a man, jet-set deb, social service-set deb, wide-eyed type, hair-up-in-rollers type. So I want to know what you're really like. What you think, what you like, what you do. You're different enough so I want to know why. Were you brought up by conventional parents or offbeat parents? Strict or permissive? Dictating or understanding?"

"I don't understand you at all," protested Wendy. "I really don't. But if you ask for a life history, you must be kook enough to listen to it."

But she couldn't find a beginning, and the silence became awkward. She was surprised at herself, because usually she could out-talk all her friends and even had a bad reputation as interrupter and talker both at the same time. She could be rude and ruthless and nonstop. But this was too much like a put-up job. Then Wendy remembered her resolution to foil whatever scheme Peter Banbury had in mind. Here was a chance. What outrageous details could she concoct? That her mother was a frustrated concert pianist or an escaped Russian ballerina? That her father was a Mr. Barrett of Wimpole Street?

But the mischief in her mind must have reflected like a blush on her face, because Peter grinned wickedly. "I'll know if you're putting me on. You have the most transparent face I've ever seen. Besides, I know you live near Westerly. Your father is quite famous for his maps."

"Is he?"

"You are an ungrateful child!"

That did it. Where flattery would have evoked small waves of false modesty or pride, words that dried up the conversation because they had nowhere to go, criticism opened up a flood of self-defense. All the reasons

Wendy had lined up to support her actions came gushing out, rushing over the background of her life as she saw it. She talked until her throat was dry. Peter listened. Occasionally he shifted in his seat. After half an hour, Wendy slowed down.

"I'm going up for a cigarette. You want one?"

"No. We smoke at school just because they frown. But I don't really like it that much. I'd rather use the money for other things—like Julian Bream records. You can bring me back a drink of water, though."

He took the zippered bag along with him, as if he didn't trust her with it. But when he came back in fifteen minutes, he had remembered her drink. She was drowsy.

"Put your head down and cork off for a while," he suggested. "We may be up all night once we get to Boston."

"But you only heard Chapter One," Wendy smirked at him. "We got to where I was thirteen and discovered boys. I'm just getting to the interesting part."

"I can't stand anyone's fumbling-and-acne period. It was bad enough going through my own. Spare me the details."

"But those are the years where you feel so *wounded* all the time! It affects your whole personality."

"I'm sure you were wounded. But I don't want to know how, what, why, where, and when."

"That sounds suspiciously journalistic. Do you mind telling me, Peter Banbury, what you're up to?"

"What do you mean? I'm not up to anything—except looking for some old friends and hopping off the treadmill for a while."

"But when you were on the phone, talking to that man at the brokerage house, you told him you had another job. What is it?"

"Nothing. I don't have any job."

"But you said—"

"I said I'd be busy. Did that imply a job? It all depends on how you interpret it."

THE PETER PAN BAG

"You don't think very much of people, do you?"

"Do you mean whether I consider their feelings? Or that I don't have the utmost respect for them?"

"I don't think you have any respect. I think you use people—ruthlessly."

"Ruthlessly! What an odd-sounding word that is. What if it were Emilylessly or Margaretlessly."

Wendy felt him turn the conversation away from himself as firmly as he would steer a car past a hole in the road. She was about to argue when she heard "Wester-LY-WESTerly—" called by the conductor.

Knowing how distinctive her long neck was, she put her head down on Peter's shoulder, trying to hunch up below the window level. He put his arm around her protectively. That gesture satisfied Wendy as the ultimate in disguise. After her mother's frequently expressed horror of the displays of affection or even ardor so casually carried on by young people in public, no family spy would ever suspect she would be the girl snuggling up to a bearded man on the train.

Her mother had once been marooned in this same double-seat setup, having to face a couple who had necked uninhibitedly all the way from New Haven.

When her mother complained, Rosalyn had pointed out, "But what business of yours was it anyway? You didn't have to sit there and stare. You could have borrowed a newspaper and read it—or taken a nap."

"But it was so embarrassing. So uncomfortable. It was even worse when my eyes were shut."

"Were they embarrassed?"

"No. Not a bit. They were absolutely insensitive to anyone around them. That's what was so infuriating."

"I don't get it," Rosalyn went on. "If they weren't aware of you, why should you get worked up about it?"

"Because living in a very crowded world is uncomfortable at times. And the only way people are going to get along with each other is with sensitivity to those around them. It really comes down to common sense, thoughtfulness, and good manners."

"Mum—you'll have to go into seclusion to survive," Rosalyn had advised her.

Then Mr. Allardyce had made his pronouncement. "I think thirty or forty years from now we'll all be tribal again. There will be too many individuals for each one to assert any individuality. So he'll have to live for a 'family' or a 'tribal' distinction."

"If there are so many people, maybe you'll have to get a license to have a baby—like people have to get licenses for cars today," suggested Annetta.

"Weird!" Dougal picked up the idea at once. "My Ninety-three convertible red-headed boy's muffler is shot. I think I'll trade him in for a brand-new Ninety-five trim-line, foam-cushioned girl."

Wendy giggled.

"What's funny?" asked Peter.

"My mother would be so shocked to see you hugging me on the train, and it reminded me of a silly family conversation." Wendy told him her father's prediction.

"Unless our generation changes a lot of ideas, your father is a prophet," Peter agreed. "There won't be individuals at all. We'll be sorted into teams or packs, and each team will have to submit to a common brain wave and common behavior in order to get along together."

"I wouldn't like that at all. I'd hate waking up and finding the tribal brain wave said all of us had to wear orange. Or all of us had to eat pizza for breakfast."

"Well, what do you think the fuss is all about now? It's rebellion against the tribal brain wave—before it's too late."

"But if that's true, why do we rush to be rebels together—in one place, or a few common places? Because when we get together, we live a communal life. And that's the first step toward the tribe." Wendy pounded Peter on the chest. "And that's just what we—really—don't—want."

"Woompfth," said Peter. "For a lily-looking girl, you hit hard. Can you remember what you just said?"

"Not too well. I could feel myself dredging it up, hauling it into shape from a very messy mind. I don't think easily."

"It was quite profound. If I repeated it to you, you'd get a swelled head and consider yourself a philosopher and be revolting to live with. But seriously, try to remember. You don't want to be just part of the tribe in the future."

"Of course not. I don't want to be just one of the crowd now."

"Now you've lost it!" Peter groaned. "There's a profound difference behind those thoughts. You're back to the trite. You've lost the feeling."

"It was only a flash. No great discovery."

"But you might need it later. A mental talisman against the darkest night."

"You talk to me for a change." Wendy rubbed her head contentedly against his shoulder, and even though his soft beard tickled her forehead ridiculously as he spoke, she didn't move. Just after Providence she fell asleep.

"Wendy!" Peter nudged her awake as the train crawled into Boston. "You've paralyzed me. I'll never get this arm working again."

"Sorry," she murmured. "I hate to wake up."

"The train's stopped. We'll get some coffee in the station. You have now arrived in Boston for an uncommon experience on Boston Common."

The station was shabby and dirty, and their luggage surrounded them awkwardly as they perched on stools at the drugstore counter. Peter ordered two grilled-cheese sandwiches with his coffee.

"But I don't like grilled cheese," said Wendy.

"Order what you want. These are both for me anyway. The first thing that makes me feel I'm off the treadmill is a grilled-cheese sandwich."

"Why?"

"One of the guys I'm looking for stayed in my pad in the Village last summer. He was a pacifist, a conscientious objector, a vegetarian, and a photographer. He lived on grilled-cheese sandwiches, yogurt, and nuts. I just got used to eating a lot of grilled-cheese sandwiches."

"Was he a good photographer?"

"Zack is the best. But he's very independent. So he's often out of work."

"Would he be strong enough to work if he lived on cheese, nuts, and yogurt?"

"You'd be surprised how much mileage you can get out of that diet."

"I'll take your word for it. How's your strength now? Are we going by subway with this stuff? Or taking a cab?"

"What kind of a hippie are you! Take a cab!"

"I never said I was a hippie. Don't put labels on people all the time. I'm not anything but me."

"I hope you memorize that."

"You know—you keep making these digs about what I say and will I remember what I said. As if it were important. Do you really think being away from home with different people in a different environment is going to destroy me? I don't. It may change me, and I think that would be good. But that's all. It's not going to defeat me."

"I should hope not. But I warn you—besides people and places, there are circumstances. Things you don't expect to change you that can change you, because they are outside forces you can't control."

"Peter, you're taking all the fun out of this with your lectures."

"Sorry. Onward and upward. We'll take a cab."

Wendy had visited Boston when she was younger and spent several school vacations with a favorite aunt who had since moved away from Brookline. So she was pre-

pared for the outspread skyline, if not for the wide
spaces of unfinished urban renewal projects. The Pru-
dential building ahead, the first real skyscraper for the
city, surprised her. Then the cab fitted itself into the
stream of traffic which took it along Charles Street, between the Public Garden and the Common. Wendy's
spirits lifted. In the open space before her, the great
elms of the Garden, distinctly patterned against the
smudged sunset, caught for a second the heart-stopping
exultation of freedom she'd felt that morning.

Then the cabdriver slowed down for a light at a cross-
walk, and Wendy heard the noise of hundreds of voices,
a different pitch of sound from the traffic. To her right,
beyond the ramp leading to the underground garage
and its truncated control building, people spilled over
the slopes of the Common, talking, arguing, singing,
moving, talking some more.

The cabdriver yawned. "Looks like a carnival, don't
it? Used to be they used the Public Garden for a festival
in the summer. Lots of culture. You know—plays and
crazy pictures. But look what's happened to Boston
Common. Nothing but a messy, dirty crowd. Pretty
sad."

The light changed and the driver concentrated on
shooting past the corner of Charles and Beacon with
the green light. "You say Sage Lane? Where's that? Up
the Hill?"

"Drop us at the corner of Myrtle. It's an alley off that."

As Peter paid off the cab, Wendy stared around her.
She'd forgotten how steep the hill was and how narrow
the streets. "I'm glad we didn't walk with all this stuff.
You need a Sherpa to carry things."

She spotted the short blind alley labeled Sage Lane.
One side was a long building with windows high in the
walls and no entrance. But the other side had a tiny
sidewalk and three narrow houses wedged tightly
against each other. A wooden fence marked the blank

end of the lane. One street light dropped a pale circle at its feet.

Peter punched the top three door buttons. Nothing happened. He tried the next. There was a series of clicks, and he swung the door back into a small hall, where a staircase immediately confronted them. But no one hollered down or seemed to be about, and to Wendy's surprise Peter didn't stop on the second floor. He led on to the third and knocked on a door at the top of the stairs. When no one came, he twisted the knob and the door opened.

"People are trusting," he said and immediately tripped over something in the dark. "Feel by the door for a light switch."

Wendy's fingers connected with one, and a bulb turned on and glowed from inside a white-pleated, Japanese paper globe, shedding light softly over a perplexing interior. What had once been two small attic rooms, with two windows at the front and the back, had been opened up into one area, leaving an old brick chimney, naked of its lath and plaster, sticking up through the middle. The walls and ceiling had been painted in a deep purple.

"It's like a cave!" said Wendy. "It should feel kind of dark and cool. But it doesn't. It's as hot here as it was in New York at noon."

"Don't complain. You could be out on the street to-night looking for a roof."

Peter stuck his head behind the doors of the two closetlike areas that served as kitchenette and bathroom.

"Someone still lives here and has had eggs for breakfast and has dyed some material which is now dripping green drips all over the shower stall."

"Who is someone?"

"I hope it's Oriana."

"Oriana what?"

"She prefers just Oriana. Like a goddess, she says she

doesn't need a last name. Did you ever hear Aurora brought down to earth as Miss Aurora Dewsnap? Or meet a Miss Ariadne Fink?"

"I'm suspicious. Is she a cultist or a schizo?"

"Neither. She's just a rather unpredictable and very individual female."

Wendy was so fascinated with the apartment's weird atmosphere that she didn't bother to defend her sex against Peter's opinion.

There were two studio couches against the wall, haphazardly covered with old chenille bedspreads that were home-dyed to an uneven crimson. The cushion backs of the couches were placed together on the floor and covered by a third dyed spread. There were no chairs. Peter had tripped over an enormous red-leather hassock, which must once have been considered a prize. Now its soft leather was faded and cracked, and the embroidered Turkish designs coming out thread by thread. On the floor was a dark gritty rug. Wendy resolved to keep her sandals on. On one wall was a large poster with a complicated symbolic design in colors that made her blink.

"You'll be all right. I'm going to stay on the floor below. Zack is there. He's renting a friend's place for the summer. Anyway, I have an errand to do that may take me a couple of hours. But I'll stick my head in the door and say 'Hi' when I come back."

But Wendy didn't want to be dumped and left in this odd cave with no one to talk to. "I'm not at all sleepy now. I'll come with you."

"I don't think that would be such a good idea."

"Peter, you are up to something! You can't deny it."

"Of course!" Peter laughed. "I'm going out to rescue the Lost Boys from Captain Hooked and bring them home so you can mend their pockets."

6

PETER FIRMLY CLOSED the door, leaving Wendy frustrated and furious. "Don't forget your stupid shadow!" she yelled after him. "I wish J. M. Barrie had choked on his treacle."

His footsteps stopped on the floor below and someone greeted him. In a few minutes, she heard him leave the building, talking quietly, and a man's voice replying. From the window she watched Peter and another fellow walk quickly out of Sage Lane. She sat down on the hassock, which sank unevenly beneath her, nearly tipping her onto the dirty rug. The poster on the wall picked at her nerves. *If I stare at it, it will hypnotize me*, she thought. She squinted at it cautiously, and through her lashes the room seemed even more cavelike, but with an odd familiarity that bothered her. Suddenly she realized it reminded her of the set in *Peter Pan* where the Lost Boys lived underground. *How am I going to make Peter stop this unfortunate Never-Never business if I can't get away from it myself!* she scolded herself.

Wendy's consolation was her lute. She undid the case, tuned it, and then sat cross-legged on the backless couch, forgetting herself with music. Her voice was clear and true, and she enjoyed singing, so much so that she jumped when someone said, "Hullo! What are you doing here!"

A girl had quietly opened and closed the door, but there was no warmth or friendliness in her study of Wendy, just a kind of sullen suspicion.

"Are you Oriana?" Wendy asked. "A friend of mine who knows Oriana left me here to stay with her."

"Oriana isn't here. I don't know when she'll be back."

"Oh, dear!" Wendy hopped off the couch. "You certainly don't want to take in a friend of a friend of a friend who isn't here."

"It doesn't bother me. People come and go. I don't care who knows who and who doesn't. Is it important who knows you?"

"I guess not," Wendy said, uneasily, even though the girl, still staring at her, made her feel as welcome as a bad cold. "Look, I won't stay if you don't want me. But I do have to wait until my friend comes back. He went off with someone downstairs."

"Don't flap." The girl came on into the room. "If you stay out of my hair and don't expect to be babied or waited on, you can do as you please. Oriana pays the rent anyway."

"Where is she?"

"She's in Vermont. Goddessing."

"You're not serious! Nobody is a goddess today. Or do you mean she has a job? Like goddess instead of waitress?"

"It's no job. It's just what she is—when she's with this particular group of people. They live on a farm, but they speak of it as a temple."

"Oh? I suppose it's all the same. I mean, whether you go off to meditate with a guru and go through all the Hare Krishna bit, or whether you put yourself into a universal attitude by saying 'Om.' Or whether you—can be a goddess. It's whatever your own thing is. Right?"

"Exactly. Respect your own and don't knock other people's."

The girl's dark blond hair was coarse and hung around her shoulders in a long shaggy Dutch cut. Despite the heat, she wore Indian-squaw moccasins, heavy bell-bottomed jeans, a sort of tunic-blouse which looked old and shiny, and a large flat ornamental necklace beaded with a pattern of Indian peace symbols. She went to one of the couches and lay down.

"You can go on playing that thing if you like. I don't mind."

Wendy couldn't think of anything she'd rather do than play her lute to comfort herself in an uneasy situation. But she disliked being told what she could or could not do, and this remote girl was far from Wendy's expectation of the kindness and communal warmth supposed to be typical of the Village or Haight-Ashbury and similar gathering places. But then—Boston and New England were known for being frosty.

"Are you from Boston?" Wendy asked.

"Hardly." The girl closed her eyes and shut Wendy out. Maybe the frost even rubbed off on transients.

Wendy wondered what time it was, and how long it would be before Peter came back. Ordinarily she would have hauled out her watch and checked, but she was uneasy about scrabbling around in her knapsack and hauling out a gold watch.

So Wendy perched again on the couch, cross-legged. She didn't sing, but she plonked at the lute absentmindedly, giving the strings a tweak now and then, when her thoughts needed punctuating. She tried to keep her eyes off the dizzying poster and her mind from panicking. *After all,* she told herself, *you've had a confusing day. You're still trying to rationalize your actions because it's so new being responsible just to yourself and this is quite different. But you haven't given it a chance yet. Even the most looked-forward-to, dreamed-about thing is usually a letdown the first time you see it. You can't feel at home and comfortable and free until you've lived here a while. And you are not home-*

*sick. Not one little bit. Repeat after me. Om, Om,
Ommmmmm. Forget familiar faces and wondering
what they're doing and if they miss you. Om, Om. Repeat after me: This is an adventure. I am free of my
smothering family, and that's what I want. This adventure, this life, is all mine. Om, Om, Om.*

Her knowledge of the Om phenomenon came from a
lecture in Comparative Religion at school. The girls
had gone around chanting "Om" for kicks and several
of them, in need of an image, had worked at it seriously
for some weeks until they were bored. But way back in
Wendy's prodigious amount of reading there was another aspect of Om which tugged at her mind with a
rather horrible meaning. She plucked at the lute, until
it came to her with the same impact as when she'd first
read it in *A Passage to India*. It was the horror, the stark
terror of the old lady alone in the dark Mirabar Caves,
where all the evil of the world seemed to wrap around
her in the unceasing resounding sound of Om. Wendy
shivered. This cavelike room with its crushingly dark
walls was bugging her to a horror point, too. What was
it Peter had said about outside forces she couldn't control? It was silly. She could take it or leave it alone.
She was in control of herself; she was not a collapsed
quivering old lady shuddering in a Mirabar Cave.

She sat up straight, flung an arpeggio over the lute
strings and sang,

> This great World is a Trouble
> Where all must their Fortunes bear,
> Make the most of the Bubble,
> You'll have but Neighbour's Fare:
> Let not Jealousy teize ye,
> Think of nought but to please ye;
> What's past, 'tis but in vain
> To wish for the Time again.

"Encore," said a voice. Again she was startled to find
someone had come into the room while she was singing.

"Once again—" said the young man by the door.

"This great World is a Trouble," sang Wendy, and he added a tenor melody, improvising it, but keeping it in the right eighteenth-century spirit. They ended it together in harmony and grinned at each other in satisfaction.

"I'm Zack," he said and sat down beside her. "Peter told me to come keep you company awhile. What a beautiful instrument that is! May I?"

She handed him the lute, and he turned it about, admiring its shape and the grain of the wood, as well as its tone.

"I'm so glad to meet you," Wendy said. "It seemed very oppressive in here."

"I know what you mean." Zack nodded toward the girl on the couch, who hadn't moved and barely seemed to breathe. She looked as pallid and lifeless as Juliet after taking the potion.

"Is she all right?" Wendy asked.

"Sure. Probably just coming down from a high. She's like four or five different people anyway, depending on what stage she's in of whatever kick she's on. Sometimes she can be your good friend and ten hours later act as if she'd never met you."

"What's her name?"

"Jez. Or Jezzy. I think it began as plain Jessie from New Jersey. But she'd rather shock you into thinking it's short for Jezebel. Just mind your own business and do your own thing, and she'll ignore you most of the time."

"She says Oriana is away."

"That's right. She's been away about a week. Anyone who has connections in the country right now is smart. Boston's getting sticky, weather-wise and fuzz-wise. What a picture Jez makes like that! Not exactly the Sleeping Beauty. More like the Sleeping Sphinx. People are mysterious when they're asleep. Be back quicker than a flashbulb. Just keep on with that lute, soothingly. So she doesn't move."

"I don't think she'd hear the roof blow off."

Zack was back with a camera and flashbulbs before Wendy even decided what she felt like singing. Zack moved quietly around, as Wendy bent over the lute, re-tuning it, and began an old ballad about "Robin Hood and the Stranger." It had many verses, for it told a complete story, and Wendy prided herself on having learned them all. At first the bulbs startled her, and then she became absorbed in the ballad and didn't even wince when they went off. Jez seemed unaware of either light or sound and didn't stir. Zack, moving around the room and shooting from all angles, some of which seemed to include Wendy and some didn't, finally used up his bulbs, snapped the camera into its case, and sat down.

Wendy finished the ballad:

> And we'll be three of the bravest outlaws
>   That are in the North Countree.
> If you will have more of bold Robin Hood
>   In other tales it shall be.

"Don't stop," he said, as she put the lute down.

"Ballads always leave me breathless. They go on and on so. You'll have to talk to me till I recover. All I know is that you are a photographer, among other things."

"What other things?"

"According to Peter, you're a pacifist. A CO. And a vegetarian. I expected someone weirdish-looking."

"How?"

"Oh, with fanatic eyes and a dedicated way of speaking. And emaciated. You're not."

"Hardly. I'll be alive and enjoying myself at ninety-three when all my present contemporaries have died of heart attacks in their fifties from eating animal fats. Some of the healthiest, longest-lived people in the world just eat rice and vegetables."

"It may be healthy. But it must be boring."

"Why? Half the so-called pleasure of eating is psychological. So if you eat rice, you don't have to think rice. Think about anything you want."

"Peter said you were a great photographer, but you didn't make much money at it."

"He believes in telling the truth, doesn't he!" But Zack shrugged. "If you want to earn a real living with a camera, you work on the staff of a paper or a magazine and your assignments come from above. You do what someone else says—from photographing fashion models to city litter—and you do it against a deadline, and someone else edits the pictures. I don't want to work that way. A good photograph should have as much to say as an essay, but without ever needing words for a caption. That's what I want to do. And if I take a hundred pictures to get one perfect one, I want to decide which ninety-nine to throw away. It gets picky. You can sell free-lance—a single picture or a series on a subject. But until you're a very big name, you don't make a living from it."

"So how do you make a living?"

"Look, Peter tells me you came along with him on the spur of the moment because you walked out at home and you want to see the world. Older generations might have called it "slumming," condescending to see how the other half lives."

"That's not it at all—" Wendy interrupted.

"I didn't say that's your attitude. Maybe you do really want to experience other ways of life. But if you go around here asking people how they make a living you'll get nowhere. Ask what they think or how they feel. Then you'll get what my old guidance counselor at high school claimed he always aimed for: gut rapport." Zack made a face and then grinned. He was slight and rather tense. He walked quickly. His light-brown hair whipped up off his forehead emphatically when he talked, and there were earnest lines that crinkled around his eyes. He had a drooping but neat mustache.

He's not as young as Peter, Wendy decided, *but I can't really tell how old he is.*

Zack went on. "You'll find that what people do around here most is *talk*. By the hour. Some sing. You've got a good refuge in that, you know. Some smoke this and that. Some take trips. Some sleep alone. Some don't. But nobody goes around making statements or judgments about anybody else. It's not up to you to judge what a person does or doesn't do. Or what anyone's relationship to anyone else is. Get it?"

"Got it." Wendy put her head back against the wall with an unexpected bang.

"Tired?"

"Umm." Wendy almost choked on a yawn.

"I'll pop downstairs. I want to develop these pictures anyway. Shall I tell Peter you couldn't keep your eyes open?"

"Please. Tell him I'll see him in the morning."

"One more thing. Some people don't have too fine a distinction over what belongs to others and what they think they have a right to use for their own good. Put that lute out of sight when you're not using it."

"Oh. Thanks." Wendy's puzzlement was obvious.

"What's the matter?"

"It's all so different from what I thought. I'd heard everyone took care of everyone else. You know, shared things. I didn't expect it was so—sort of every man for himself and never mind anyone else, which it seems to be."

"You have a lot to discover. People are always people first, whether they're classed as hippies or suburbanites. There are very genuine hippies—the ones whose goodness and beliefs and motives are as pure as can be. They are concerned for the welfare of others and the beliefs of the world. They are the true and the great. But they're rare. There are maybe four or five places here or in Cambridge or Roxbury that started with a concerned group of people living together and helping others, and they're the example of what 'hippie' originally meant. They could be absorbed happily and usefully into any community for the good of all. If the community wouldn't make judgments. But then you get a circle around that center—the imitators. They use this way of life as an excuse for not making it in other ways, and they're apt to be far less concerned with helping others. It gets selfish about there. Then you get the on-lookers, the plastic hippies and weekend hippies, who want to look the part because it's in. Or want some action, but without the consequences. And then last of all, there's the punks who want to find any action and stir it up for kicks or make use of it in some way. So, you'll find all kinds. Jez is only one sample. When Oriana comes back, you'll find she's something else!"

Wendy yawned again. Zack smiled and left. Wendy put the lute in the case but left it on the floor by the couch. She locked the door, stripped off her jeans and jersey and her bikini underwear, found a short cotton nightshift in her rucksack, turned out the Japanese light and lay down on the couch. It was a long time before she fell asleep. The heat was inescapable. She wasn't used to traffic noises and voices from the streets or to sirens and fire engines and ambulances screaming their way through the city. But finally she drifted off into a sweaty sleep.

A banging on the door and rattling of the doorknob woke her with a heart-thudding start. She couldn't remember where she was and sat up on the couch, groaning. Someone outside was kicking at the door. Wendy didn't know what to do. She remembered noticing when she'd locked it that there wasn't any bolt or chain on the door, and her city-aunt had always advocated having both. She sat there, dazed.

The noise finally penetrated to Jez's consciousness, and she rose off the couch. In the light from the front windows, Wendy saw her stalk stolidly to the door and unlock it. Three figures came in.

"What's the idea, locking the door!" a girl complained. She stood by Jez, talking loudly and rather disjointedly. The other two, even in that dim light, found the couch backs on the floor and, as if they had often used them, lay down without a word.

Suddenly Jez snapped on the light, revealing Wendy sitting up on the couch.

"That was a very dumb thing to do," Jez said to her. "You shut out my friends."

"I'm sorry. You didn't say anything about expecting anyone."

"I don't ever *expect* anyone. But my friends know they are welcome. I never lock my door."

Wendy wanted to say, "It's Oriana's door. Not yours." But a tone in Jez's voice warned her.

Jez didn't bother to introduce her friends. She turned her back on Wendy and went on talking to the girl. The girl wore a long skirt, that looked as if she'd sewn it up from tarnished silver-brocade upholstery material, and a lace jacket of the Gibson-girl era, tight-boned collar and all. Strings of beads hung over the front and the girl had made some attempt to wad her long hair into the Gibson style. But the effect was far more of a child haphazardly dressing up than that of a real costume. Jez and the girl, whose name was apparently Charlene, sat on the couch and talked. Jez made no move to turn out the light, but Wendy decided not to complain. Waking up and rapping with friends at any hour was apparently one of one's things.

Then her glance took in the pair on the cushions on the floor. One already had fallen asleep, mouth open and askew, face ashen in that light, and breathing heavily. Dressed in blue jeans and a denim shirt, Wendy suddenly realized the size of the bare dirty feet gave him away, despite the rough, blondish shoulder-length hair. It was a boy. And so was the figure next to him, now that she stared, although the features were more delicate, and again, the hair, wavy brown, was shoulder-length. Wendy was suddenly aware of her thin cotton shift. *But who cares what you wear or you don't wear?* she told herself. *You shouldn't be hung-up on how you're brung-up.*

She lay down and turned her back on Jez and Charlene, trying to shade her eyes from the light and trying to shut out the voices so she could sleep.

For a while the words droned on, all to do with some other girls' problems after an encounter with the police. "Fuzzy pigs" was the comment from Jez, prefaced by several Anglo-Saxon words. And in dreary tones the other girl repeated the same, changing only to "Piggy fuzz." Then Wendy heard Charlene ask, "Where'd *she* come from?"

"Someone downstairs brought her. She thought Oriana was here, although she doesn't know her."

"*She* doesn't look the type."

"Plastic. She won't stay. She'll get scared. Or want a hot bath and go home. I'll bet her parents have a dragnet out for her already. I'll bet she lasts about one week."

Charlene grumbled about having to sleep on the floor and then suddenly pulled one of the boys off the couch cushions and onto the rug with a thud. He didn't even wake, and Charlene took his place.

Jez turned out the light. Wendy finally fell asleep again.

7

WHEN WENDY WOKE she had no idea of the time of day.
The light outside just seemed hot and intense. The four
others in the room still sprawled in sleep, remote and
unknown to her. It struck Wendy as ironic to be so in-
timately surrounded by people and yet feel so much
alone.

She took her jeans and shirt into the small bathroom.
It looked and smelled as if no one had cleaned it in
weeks. Wendy held her breath and dressed with speed.
Before she washed her face, she washed out the dirty
basin. She wondered whether the dwellers in the apartment were too busy to bother with ordinary comfort
and cleanliness or whether their professed freedom automatically included freedom from housework, and
since no one took the responsibility, nothing was done.
The trouble with you, Allardyce, Wendy told herself,
*is that you're making judgments. You're comparing
again. If you want to escape your home and that way
of life, don't go judging by it. These people have become accustomed to living this way, and it doesn't
bother them. So don't let it bother you.*

But her stomach flipped over again when she stepped
into the closetlike kitchen. There were only a few cups

and saucers around, all unwashed. Someone had attempted a stew, burned it, and the blackened contents were ripening fast in a kettle on the stove. Wendy emptied it down the toilet before the smell made her throw up. She washed the dishes in water as hot as she could stand and rather than use the one stained dish towel, stacked them in a rack to dry. The small refrigerator contained a bottle of obviously sour milk, and various little dishes of unappetizing leftovers. No eggs. No bacon. Wendy realized she was desperately hungry. Then she saw tea bags and bread and a toaster. She put water on to boil, popped two slices of bread into the toaster, and suddenly remembered the cheese in her rucksack.

Stepping into the living room, she found one of the boys crouching by her lute.

"Coo!" he said, "and gor'blimey. Is that yours?"

"Yes, it is," Wendy told him firmly. "And I treasure it and use it constantly."

"Warning to keep my filthy fingers off it, luv?"

He gave her a calculating stare and then stood up. No wonder his grubby feet had seemed so large! They matched the rest of him, which was huge. His straight blondish hair swinging over his wide shoulders reminded Wendy of illustrations of Vikings, or Siegfried in Wagner's *Ring Cycle*. But not quite. Something was missing. Arms that large around should vibrate with power, but the muscular areas hung, their resilience gone limp. Wendy sensed that though he was big, his strength was the strength of pasteboard. His blue eyes were bloodshot.

"I must say it's nice to see a new face around here," he said. "I'm Rolf. Who are you, luv?"

"Wendy." She braced herself for a comment. "Wendy" seemed to have such a built-in label now, of all the things she was trying to forget. *Too bad I didn't start out fresh and give a new name to the doorman and to Peter!* she thought. *What a lot of hang-ups that would have eliminated.* But it was too late now. Luckily, the name had no special significance one way or another to Rolf.

"Who's that on the floor?" Wendy asked.

"Charlene—and Robbie. They'll sleep all day. I'm hungry. What is there to eat?"

Wendy was surprised at his calm assumption that she would somehow provide his breakfast.

"I was about to find some cheese."

"Good girl."

He stretched and his hands almost hit the ceiling. Then he wandered into the bathroom and shut the door. Wendy scrabbled quickly through her rucksack. The cheese was limp and ripe from the heat, and she decided it might taste better as grilled-cheese sandwiches, even if she didn't really like them. She was sizzling them in a frying pan when Rolf stepped into the kitchen, and his bulk blocked the whole room.

She took the cover off the pan. He forked both sandwiches onto a plate, picked up the mug of tea she'd made, and went into the other room without even a "thanks"—all before she could say, "Stop! That's for me."

She started over again, this time hovering between the door and the stove, so he couldn't reach past her. When it was ready, she stood by the sink and gulped it down, finishing just as Rolf came back, licking greasy fingers.

"First good food since Oriana left." He smiled and dumped his dishes in the sink.

"Did Oriana do all the cooking? And the cleaning?" asked Wendy indignantly.

"I guess so. You know how it is," he said vaguely. "We all pitch in."

As Wendy washed off her plate and cup and saucer, she doubted how much pitching in Rolf ever did. Then she shrugged and washed up his dishes, too. It was too small a bother to be cross about. She wandered into the living room and felt uncomfortable. *What do you do*

*while people are sleeping around you? What is there
to do in an attic-room on a hot day in Boston?*

Rolf pulled the hassock close to the front window and
sat, looking idly down into Sage Lane. He opened a
package of ZigZag cigarette papers and shook some
dried and crumbling leaves from a Band-Aid can onto
a paper.

"Ach!" he said in disgust, as he'd shaken in the last
bit and saw it would make a very flappy cigarette.
"What a time to run out." He saw Charlene's elaborate
carpetbag which she carried to complete her costume
and didn't hesitate to look through it. He found a cigarette, broke it open, and added the tobacco to his
paper, licked and sealed it, lighted the cigarette and
leaned dreamily on the sill, smoking. After several
puffs, he offered it to Wendy. "Share a joint? Best way
to start the day."

Wendy had tried pot twice before. All it did was burn
her throat. It hadn't given her a single peek at an exciting vision. She wanted to try it again, but somehow not
now—not right after breakfast, not with what she
thought was a whole day ahead of her, and not to share
it, right from the still-greasy lips of a boy she wasn't
in the least bit thrilled by.

"No thanks. Not right now, anyway. It's too early."

"You'll get over that. Once you've been here a while,
you'll lose all that hang-up about night and day and
brushing your teeth after meals and going to bed at
night. Who says we have to do things at any certain
time?"

"Nobody," Wendy agreed. "But it does kind of get
things done and out of the way if you do them and get
them over with."

"You missed the point. You must really be up-tight.
What things in any given twenty-four hours *have* to be
done?"

"You have to eat and sleep, don't you?"

"Maybe. Maybe not. Every twenty-four hours should

be different. You should never think of day or night or twenty-four hours in one day. As long as you have it, time should be timeless. I like that. Time should be timeless," he repeated. Then he smoked quietly, and Wendy recognized the sweetish smell of the pot. Rolf put his arms on the sill and his head on his arms and ignored her.

Wendy was bored. Maybe she should have joined Rolf in a joint and the boredom would have disappeared. She decided to finish reading *Bell Call*. But before she'd turned more than a few pages, Peter Banbury knocked lightly and quietly opened the door.

"Hi." He beckoned to her, and she started to leave when she became aware of Rolf's turning to watch her. Jez also suddenly sat up. Wendy bent to pick up her rucksack. She just didn't trust either of them.

"Hello, hello, hello," Peter said cheerily. "Good day to all. I'm borrowing Wendy for a bit, but she'll be back. Bring your lute, will you? Zack and I are in need of a serenade."

"Hello, Peter. Don't rush away," said Jez. Wendy was surprised that Jez smiled and also that she knew Peter. She seemed like a different person this morning. There was a rough-and-tumble vitality about her and even her voice sounded different.

"Don't keep Wendy away long. We never did talk and get acquainted last night. How is Zack? I haven't seen him for days."

"But he was here last night!" exclaimed Wendy. "Right here in this room. He was even taking pictures of you. But—I guess you were sound asleep."

Jez smiled, but this time the smile went Sphinxlike and cold. "I was quite tired out last night. And you can tell Zack that's unfair. He knows I don't like to pose for pictures awake or asleep. So he needn't bother to develop them."

"I'll give him the message. Come on, Wendy." Peter

picked up her lute, and she followed him with the ruck-sack.

The two rooms of the apartment Zack sublet had been joined into one by as large an opening as possible in the middle wall. But they were a happy contrast to Oriana's weird decoration. The walls were clean and whitewashed. Two dark-covered studio couches had small pillows in flamboyant colors along the back. The floor was bare wood. A mobile of odd-shaped, gaily enameled pieces hung from the ceiling and the lights and hanging lamps had heavy white Danish paper shades circling them. Wendy couldn't help wishing Peter had let her stay here overnight, in what was a much less depressing atmosphere. But she supposed it was because she'd fussed about staying in 12-C with him, so he'd left her—supposedly—with a girl, Oriana.

There was very little furniture, so the rooms seemed both spacious and tidy, although Wendy noticed Peter's zipper bag, half-open, right in the middle of the sturdy coffee table.

"Coffee and scrambled eggs coming up," Peter announced, as he motioned for her to park on the couch by the table.

"You'll laugh. But I just had a grilled-cheese sandwich."

"You must have been desperate."

"I was. What time is it, anyway?"

"Two o'clock in the afternoon. That's why I went up —to see if you were still alive."

"Rolf was right. Time doesn't really matter after all, once you let go of it." Wendy was amazed but couldn't quite relax with the idea that she'd lost half a day.

"How is it up there? I didn't realize Jez had men camping overnight," Peter said. "But you did refuse to camp along with me, you know."

"I know." Wendy took the coffee from Zack, who nodded a greeting and went back to fetch the eggs. "Well, it's interesting up there. I can't figure things out though. I mean I can't figure out what kind of people they all are."

"You shouldn't lump them all into a bunch and say 'they.' Because they're all different people," said Zack.

"True. And I shouldn't tell you first impressions then, because they're probably not fair."

"Why not tell me?" asked Peter. "Then you can throw away the first impressions and go on to something else. That's one of the stupidest hang-ups people have—that you immediately find out what someone is all about and then he stays just that way so you always understand him. Everyone changes—all the time."

"I don't think that's true," Wendy argued. "I think your first impression can be wrong, but once you do find out what a person is like, he doesn't change much one way or another."

Half an hour later they finished the argument amicably, and in the process of it, Peter pulled rather vivid impressions out of Wendy on everything she'd experienced since her arrival the night before. Zack wandered in and out, putting a fresh film in one of his cameras and taking a shot unexpectedly of Wendy with her mouth wide open, arguing madly. When she protested, he laughed. "Sometimes the first couple of frames don't even come out."

"I'll bet that one does, just out of sheer spite."

"You make a good subject," said Zack. "Almost as good as Oriana."

"Will you *please* tell me about Oriana. Everyone talks about her continually."

"And everyone speaks of her differently. You'll have to wait and see for yourself." Peter stood up. "Now—do you want to wander around town for a while with me?"

"Sure. Zack, do you mind if I leave my things here? Or don't you lock up either?"

"I lock. I've got too much valuable camera and darkroom equipment to take chances."

When they came out of Sage Lane, Peter set out

briskly. "A few years ago you'd have been rigorously frowned at for wearing jeans and a jersey on Beacon Hill. But the old natives are used to seeing all kinds of people and all kinds of clothes around here now. In fact, you rarely see the old natives."

Wendy wished Peter would slow down a little, but he was scowling and thinking about something. He hiked rapidly and she scuttled after him, her leather sandals slipping on the worn brick sidewalk. Finally, as he cut through Louisburg Square, she said, "Whoa! Or are you challenging me to a race?"

"Sorry." He stopped abruptly and gave her a chance to catch her breath and look around at the small but famous square. It was really a rectangle of houses, surrounding an iron-fenced narrow strip of grass bearing tall trees. Side by side, the houses of warm brick, some with windows set in rounded bays, some with fancy iron balconies, preserved the dignity of Old Boston. But there was an air of desertion, especially on a hot summer afternoon.

"Zack says just run down the hill from here to Charles Street—about two blocks—and you've got the whole gamut of gaps. Not just the generation gap, but the abyss between rich and destitute, rooted and restless, stolid old cold-roast Boston and transients from everywhere. He says it fascinates him, and he's trying to do a picture essay on it. He's out prowling with his camera at all hours."

They hiked up Mount Vernon Street and down Walnut to cross Beacon to the Common. The shallow, stone-rimmed Frog Pond was full of kids wading and splashing in tepid water that smelled of chlorine. A few mothers of very little children sat on benches. But older children seemed to be completely on their own or in gangs. At the far end Wendy noticed some hippies, sitting on the edge, cooling their feet. While she watched, one girl stepped in, crouched to her shoulders in the water and tipped her head back until her long hair floated out in a dark fan. Then she shook like a dog and settled down again—hair, shirt, and bell-bottoms all dripping and cool.

Peter stopped walking and studied the group, who were quiet and paying attention only to themselves, even when kids deliberately splashed them.

"What would you do if someone splashed you?" Peter asked thoughtfully.

"I'd splash back!" said Wendy, thinking of the wild water rows she had in the Wallow with Dougal and Ian.

"Why?"

"For revenge! Or just plain for the rowdy fun."

"What strikes you about that little group?"

"Maybe they're tired. Maybe they're lazy. Maybe they're stoned into stone. Anyway, they're too solemn. It looks more like some kind of rite than a good time."

"It does remind you of the Ganges. People hopefully immersing themselves in filthy river water and expecting all kinds of blessings from it. I expect the Frog Pond bestows a small amount of cool and a large amount of athlete's foot."

At the top of a little hill, Peter leaned against the base of a statue which seemed to be symbolizing all kinds of different things at once. Four hefty allegorical ladies stared with granite scowls, each in a different direction, and one flight up, so to speak, other allegorical ladies earnestly clutched their heavy drapery. Above them rose a slim stone column, topped by an eagle.

Wendy saw a young boy stretched out on the grass, staring up at the eagle as if it hypnotized him. The trees around the knoll cast down a good shade, and young people lay around, dreaming, sleeping, smoking, chatting, or just silently enduring the heat. The unshaded slopes of the Common down to Charles Street were almost empty.

Peter started off again and led across to the Public Gardens, where the trees spread out more and gave more circles of shade.

"Let's ride on a Swan Boat!" Wendy dug in her pocket for a quarter.

Peter gave her a look. "In this heat? You'd feel like a crouton floating on a bowl of hot soup!"

"But if you're doing something, then you don't feel as hot." Wendy found herself quoting one of her father's favorite expressions, and despite all her intentions of independence, she felt a sudden catch of loneliness. Her father always had a didactic answer for everything. She forgot she'd never agreed with him about keeping busy to feel cooler.

"You go. I'll watch."

"All right," Wendy decided. "I will."

A boy took her fare, and she stepped onto the empty boat waiting at the dock. It carried five rows of green benches on a low catamaranlike hull. On the back was a huge white swan, in which sat another boy who pedaled the craft around the pond. Wendy roasted on the front bench, but there was no rush of passengers. She saw Peter lying under a tree sharing the shade with a family of ducks smart enough to climb out of the hot water in the pond.

How sensible Peter is, Wendy thought. *I can't believe for one minute he's a true hippie. He's not even pseudo or plastic. There's someone and something he reminds me of. I wish my mind weren't so stuck together in this heat. I wonder if it's cooler in Zack's apartment. I wonder if I could sort of stay with them tonight. Maybe I could just fall asleep on the floor there. They wouldn't wake me up and make me go upstairs. Peter has some purpose parking me up there, and I wish I knew what it was.*

Finally a weary family of tourists sagged onto the boat, and the swan-fellow took off on a stately tour. Swans and ducks hardly bothered to swim out of the way as they passed under the small suspension bridge and round the other half of the pond. The family chattered and took pictures. One child bent over to trail a hand and stare seriously down into the gloomy water. His earnest look reminded Wendy of Ian contemplating his ant farm with scientific scrutiny.

That's what Peter observing the hippies reminds me of! Scientific scrutiny! thought Wendy, and tucked the idea into her mind to consider later when it was cooler.

Peter met her at the dock, and they crossed Charles Street again to the Common. "The action doesn't get going until later on these hot days, I guess," said Peter. "I'll come back in the evening. Most of my friends from last summer are supposed to be around. I'm curious to see how they're making out."

They crossed Beacon and onto Charles and Wendy was fascinated by the shops—small groceries, flower shops, several bookstores, some specialty clothing stores, and many antique and secondhand shops. She saw some old earrings in the corner of a window.

"Peter! I've got to go in!" She started down the steps to the basement shop, when she saw Jez hurrying toward them. Jez seemed delighted to see them.

"Good news!" Jez exclaimed. "Oriana is back. Come help me pick out some pomegranates for her." She pulled them into a fruit store so enthusiastically that Wendy forgot the earrings. But when they came out, she started once again down the steps to the shop.

"Oh, don't go in there," Jez said. "He's a real pain. He charges three times what something's worth and buys it for nothing—and complains all the time."

Wendy hesitated. "I just want to ask how much those earrings are."

Jez unexpectedly put a hand on Wendy's arm and tugged at her. "But you can do that any time. Oriana's anxious to meet you."

Jez imparted that sentence as if it were an unquestioned command. It intrigued Wendy. After all, she had come in hope of unique new friendships that would make her life more exciting more meaningful. Peter seemed to be putting himself outside her experience by being an observer rather than a participant. Zack intrigued her, but he was not a relaxed hippie. Jez puzzled her. Rolf repelled her. Perhaps Oriana would become the friend she needed.

8

WENDY FELT a difference the minute she stepped into the apartment. Cushions were back on the couches. The rug had been swept so it didn't crunch underfoot. There was no trace of Charlene or Rolf and Robbie.

She rather expected to find Oriana sitting serenely in a lotus position before the hypnotic poster on the wall. She was not prepared for the small, slight girl who emerged from the bathroom wringing a cleaning cloth out in ammonia water. A shiningly clean girl, too. Her long black hair was pulled into a gleaming twist at her neck. Her scrubbed face was untouched by makeup except for black lines drawn across her eyelids, emphasizing her large dark eyes that hinted slantingly of some Tartar or Mongol centuries ago in her family history. Her face was light-skinned, pale, and thin enough to show her strong cheekbones. She was well proportioned, but not delicate. She wore what looked like an old gym tunic—and it was her favorite color, purple.

"Hullo. I'm Oriana," she said briskly, not waiting for Jez to introduce them. "You're Wendy. Peter! How choice to see you." She stepped airily up to Peter and held up her face to be kissed.

He gave her a wary salute on the cheek. "I see you're

back from the country full of clean resolution and purpose."

"I'll miss the fresh, pure air tonight! It is so foolish for people to clot together in cities—in such smudge and smirk. But when I'm up there in the fresh air, I go frantic for the smudgy, smirky people in the smudgy, smirky city."

Wendy was immediately intrigued by Oriana. She felt tuned toward her mind, as she had toward Peter's. But Oriana, at least, had no ulterior motive and was meeting her as a potential friend—not as an innocent but useful bird.

Jez presented the pomegranates. Oriana was pleased and admired them while Wendy found a clean plate for them. Oriana put the plate on the hassock.

"Don't you want one now?" Jez urged.

"In good time," Oriana promised. "I want to finish the polishing before my friend arrives. One doesn't scuttle around him. One sits and is absorbed."

"Expecting the Maharishi, eh?" cracked Peter.

"Hardly." Oriana frowned. "He was a fad."

"What! Centuries of Eastern scrutiny and meditation summed up in one holy man is a fad?"

"That's just it, Peter. *One* holy man is a fad. The centuries of wisdom are not. No, I am expecting my friend William. He is my mentor now, you know. He has really helped me find myself. I have the deepest respect for his judgment and values."

"Mentor seems an awesome description of William, if he's the fellow you ended up with in the Village last summer," said Peter. Wendy got the feeling Peter was not being an remote observer this time. He was involved.

"Just because you didn't like him, Peter, you don't need to ridicule him."

"I don't *dis*like him. I just don't have the patience to sit and listen to him run off at the mouth."

"Do you have a Ph.D.?" Oriana asked.

"No."

"William does. So do three of his friends at the farm. It was very intense and immensely interesting while I was there. William is only coming to the city for two or three days, because he says he needs to feel the vibration of restlessness in the city to reinforce his tranquility. You are just being jealous and juvenile, Peter, and I don't want you upsetting William."

Wendy noticed that Peter flushed and cut off an angry reply with some quickly applied self-control. She suddenly realized that Peter knew Oriana very well. He might even have been in love with her, until William appeared and apparently had wiped him out.

Peter turned to Wendy. "I'll see you later." He left abruptly.

Undisturbed, Oriana stepped into the kitchen, where she had begun preparation of a rather complicated dish, using the big kettle. "Jez," she announced, "I need raisins and almonds and saffron. I don't see any left on the shelf."

"We kind of used up things while you were away."

"Then you'll have to go and get them. Now."

"Sure," Jez agreed meekly. Wendy was surprised, as she had not thought of Jez as a very compliant person.

"Do you have some money?" Jez asked Oriana.

"Ha! Never. I hitched from Vermont. I won't have any money till next week."

"Oh."

Jez stood uncertainly in the middle of the room. She looked briefly at a large old brown-leather suitcase which sat by her couch and was used as an end table to hold an ash tray. Then Jez looked at Wendy. "Are you planning to stay with us?"

"If there's room." Wendy wondered if Oriana's respect and admiration of William meant she would want the apartment uncluttered with visitors or if she wanted an audience for her guru.

"There's always room," Oriana said matter-of-factly.

"Room is a communal concept. So we share. What do you have to share?"

"I'll be glad to go out and get the groceries," said Wendy. "Just give me a list."

"Thank you."

Jez handed Oriana a pad of paper and a pencil. Oriana, after a shrewd look at Wendy, wrote a longer list than just raisins and saffron and almonds. She added celery, a five-pound chicken, onions, apples, curry, and two pounds of long-grain rice. Wendy wondered if she had anything in that big kettle on the stove besides water.

She remembered she'd left her money in the rucksack at Zack's. So she had to stop by for it. As she knocked, she thought she heard a female voice inside, talking away. But when Zack opened the door, no one else was in sight. Not even Peter, although she was sure the bathroom door had just been closed.

"Hi, there. Come in." For some reason Zack seemed embarrassed to see her. So she decided to take her things back upstairs out of his way.

"Just came for my stuff. I'm going out food-shopping for Oriana."

"Picking up the check?"

"Shouldn't I? I'm staying there."

"A contribution is okay. Just don't get stuck as the sole means of support."

"I can hardly do that. I didn't bring much money, and I'm not working."

"None of them work either," Zack warned her.

"Then how can Oriana afford the rent?"

"Her father pays it. He says he just wants to know she has a roof over her head—as long as it isn't his roof."

"Real loving father!"

"Who knows? You read about him in the paper every other day. High-level government position. I guess he couldn't have her at home and keep his job, is all. Besides she split long ago. Coming for a stroll with Peter and me later?"

"Sure. Although I think Oriana is planning a feast."

"Then count on its being ready to eat about two in the morning."

Wendy laughed. "If there's one thing I'm enjoying, it's that time doesn't matter. It takes the pressure off."

Zack smiled and handed over her lute and rucksack.

"Wait a minute." She dumped the contents of the sack on his couch and fished out two five-dollar bills and then tumbled everything back. "Thanks a heap."

Zack had been watching her carefully. "Will you pose for me? Here and there? Now and then? It suddenly occurs to me you've got the only genuine, spontaneous, outrageously cheerful smile I've seen around here in weeks! Maybe everyone else has just lost his smile or is keeping it for something funny and then doesn't find anything funny. Somedays I feel smothered by vapid faces. Vague faces locked away in dreams. That's why I was so possessed to shoot Jez last night. I thought maybe I'd find out more about her when she was honestly asleep than when she's guardedly awake."

"What do you mean guardedly awake? I thought she was being very much her naturally aggressive self all the time."

"She's the natural self she's decided to be. Here. Now. But she reminds me of a masked character in a play—and the mask makes a rigid role."

"You're so cynical! I don't know whether I should pose for you or not."

"Well, don't pose. Just don't object and make faces if I snap you. Now and then. Here and there."

"All right." Wendy ran upstairs, left her things and hurried to the store where Jez had bought the pomegranates. But she lingered, looking again at the earrings in the basement-shop window.

As she gathered her big bag of groceries, she was

appalled at her ten dollars vanishing all at once—and
into what was apparently to be only one meal. Not even
a week's food!

Charles Street was busier now than it had been all
day. People straggled home from work. Shopkeepers
carefully secured their windows and doors for the night.
Hippies who had slept away a hot, empty day strolled
out looking for connections—their friends, their contacts, some action. Hippies who had wandered through
the day and already purchased their needs were looking
for a spot for the night—a corner to talk in, smoke in,
and sleep in.

For a second Wendy thought that a girl with a rather
long full skirt approaching her was Charlene. But it
wasn't. The girl stared at Wendy's grocery bag and then
stopped right in front of her so Wendy had to stop or
bump into her.

"You look affluent," the girl said. "How about a little
something for a friend?"

"I've got an extra bunch of celery," Wendy offered
sympathetically. "Just pull it out of the bag."

"Good God! I don't mean celery. I mean, have you
got an extra joint? Or how about a quarter for a cup of
dreamy coffee or a hashish brownie? Just a quarter for
a cup of God knows what. Now do you know what I
mean?"

The initial shock of seeing a girl her own age brazenly
beg—and then hearing what she was begging for—left
Wendy with her mouth open. Finally she said in em-
barrassment, "I'm sorry. I just spent all my money on
food."

The girl's expression grew taut, but it seemed to
Wendy that her eyes reflected a tremendous weariness.
So Wendy went on, "Except for some change." She
opened her hand and showed two quarters and three
dimes. The girl grabbed it off her palm and grinned.

"I'll do the same for you someday!" she exclaimed,
tucking the money into a beaded reticule hanging over

her wrist. She reminded Wendy of the bedecked but wizened little monkey on a chain she'd seen once, collecting money in a cup for its organ-grinder master.

"Don't believe a word of it," said a voice behind Wendy. "It's Little Knocky Nell. And she's strictly a one-man panhandler."

It was Rolf, glaring at the girl in the long skirt, who flounced past him with an effect she could never have achieved in a mini-skirt. "Just because you're not the man I panhandle for, you needn't be mean, Rolf."

Rolf, his eyes on the groceries, walked along beside Wendy, but he didn't offer to carry the bag. He laughed when she stopped to ring the door button to the apartment, put his hand on the outside doorknob, and opened the door before any response came from upstairs.

"Isn't even that door locked?" asked Wendy.

"What the landlord doesn't know won't hurt him. Just a little matter of a common pin in the right spot."

"But—anyone can just get in anytime!"

"How clever you are to figure that out," Rolf said sarcastically. "But don't be afraid. The word is out only among friends. And burglars would break in anyhow. So what's to lock? Locks are only to separate space, and why should one space be separate from another when space is all that holds us apart and binds us together? Space is to people what skin is to bones. So why should one space belong to one person and not to another?"

He suddenly sat down on the stairs, blocking her way. She stood there, clutching the groceries, but waiting patiently while he tried to explain the sudden flash of his philosophy that glimmered in his brain. "One of the first trips I ever took I still remember—in infinite detail. *Infinite*. It had to do with space. You know, Einstein could probably have developed his theory of relativity on one good acid trip—instead of spending years of nit-picky thinking."

"Tell me more." Peter came down the stairs and sat on

the step behind Rolf. Wendy gave up and set the groceries on the floor and leaned on the railing.

"I'll tell you what I found out about space. Did you know that the air between a table and a chair is filled with millions of dancing particles? Like snowflakes? And you could spend your life admiring each one because it's different? On this trip I watched a thousand of them, and each one expanded to the size of a drive-in movie screen, and then each expanded design had intricate shading of light and dark, and all I had to do was tip my head to make the designs take on colors. It was like having two kaleidoscopes for eyes. But all the time I knew, I *knew*, see—that I was only beginning to explore the possibilities between that table and that chair. It was very cosmic."

"Are all your trips taken between tables and chairs?" asked Wendy, giggling a little.

"What's funny?" Rolf sent her a hurt and puzzled look.

"It just struck me as funny to feel that you'd been on an infinite cosmic trip, between a table and a chair."

"You are inexperienced, aren't you!" Rolf's look this time was pitying. "We'll have to see what we can do about that."

Wendy realized that Zack was hanging perilously over the staircase rail, taking pictures. And from the top landing, Jez yelled, "Hurry up with those groceries. Oriana needs them."

"Coming." Wendy edged past Rolf, who wanted to go on telling about his cosmic discoveries, and Peter who seemed content to sit and listen. Zack annoyed her with a flashbulb dazzling her in the face as she came on up the stairs. "You look great wreathed in celery."

"You'll be crowned with it in a minute."

"Look—dump that stuff on Oriana and come along with us now. I'd like to get some pictures on the Common before the light goes."

"Oriana may need some help."

"If she's making her famous—and only—dish, Indonesian chicken curry, that kitchen will be hotter than the food. Which is hot."

"It sounds good. And I'm hungry."

"I warn you—it won't be ready for hours. Come on, I'll treat you to a submarine sandwich."

"You win!" Wendy's stomach easily beat her limited sense of domestic obligation. She ran up the last flight and dashed in. When she saw that Jez now sat on the hassock awkwardly trying to play her lute, she was furious. She thumped the groceries down by the sink and turned back to Jez. "I'm sorry. But I don't like people to use my lute. Especially when they don't know how to handle it properly."

Jez kept on twanging at the strings, and Wendy felt embattled, just the way she used to feel when Rosalyn and Annetta ganged up on her. "I meant it!" said Wendy, bristling. She wanted to snatch it away from Jez, but it seemed such a childish thing to do.

"Oh, take it." Jez thrust it at her. Wendy became aware of Oriana watching them from the doorway. "With such a possessive attitude, you must be a spoiled only child."

"I'm not. I have two sisters and two brothers."

"You'd never know it," Jez went on. "But maybe your mother never made you share things with each other."

"Of course she did. We had to even out the Christmas chocolates and the Easter eggs—down to the last lick. But a lute is different.

"Why? Doesn't music belong to everyone? Isn't everyone free to express himself? Or is it just star performers, like you, who can?"

"Look!" Wendy was exasperated. "It seems to me you've wandered way off the point. Sharing things has nothing to do with taking good care of a treasured possession. My mother never made Dougal hand his oboe around because she thought we should all express ourselves on his oboe. Furthermore, she expects each of us to take excellent care of any musical instrument and not just dub around with it."

"What were you—a family orchestra?" Jez asked in a sour voice.

"Hardly. I don't think anyone has ever composed music for harmonica, oboe, banjo, cello, and lute! And kazoo. My father's a mean kazoo player."

Again there was a sudden twist of anxiety in her mind, but this was no time to examine it. Right now she didn't want to know if it came from missing her family. It couldn't. After all, she'd left because she couldn't stand their "parentally dictated and culturally programmed existence" any more! She remembered having hit on that description of her family while talking to Peter on the train, and she liked it too much to forget it. But then, Wendy thought, could that painful twinge come from wondering if they missed her?

She held the lute, and just feeling the warm familiar wood in her hands soothed her.

Oriana smoothed her hands down her gymlike tunic and attempted to restore harmony. "Perhaps later you can teach Jez how to play a song on your lute. Then you won't feel it's desecrated if someone borrows it. Now Jez—how about peeling some onions?"

"Are you ever coming, Wendy?" Zack stuck his head in the door.

"Do you need some help?" Wendy asked Oriana.

"Oh, no. Jez and I will cope."

"What time should I be back? When do you think you'll eat?" Wendy wanted to know.

"When it's ready," Oriana said, as if that were the only possible answer. Wendy felt like a fool. Why couldn't she let go of her old hang-ups about time and possessions? They all stood in her way and mocked her.

Zack tugged at her. "Don't stand there brooding. Peter's already outside."

Carrying the lute, she followed Zack downstairs and

out to join Peter in the lane. Rolf rose off his perch and
followed her. Without speaking, they Indian-filed down
the Hill and in and out among the people on the narrow
Charles Street sidewalk. Peter no longer wore the
heavily embossed pendant around his neck, but his
beard and longish hair drooped in the heat. Zack had
swapped to a small camera that he could use almost
inconspicuously. Wendy scowled and seemed unaware
she still clutched the lute. Rolf ambled behind, taking
long steps with his large, ugly bare feet. No one passing
by paid any attention to any of them, and suddenly
Wendy no longer felt a visitor to the scene.

She couldn't see, from what she'd discovered so far,
what all the fuss against hippie life was about. That is,
if Oriana was an example. She looked as if she were so
clean she'd squeak! Except for the continual talk, talk,
talk and the casual sleeping arrangements, it was all
quite live and let live. But there was a dim echo in
Wendy's mind as she realized almost all her hours since
leaving home had been spent in talking.

What had caught on her memory this time? Then she
remembered: *I accused my family of doing nothing but
talk!*

Wendy chuckled and nearly ran down Zack, who'd
stopped for the light at Charles and Beacon. "Don't
brain me with that lute!" he warned.

Once across the street, she hurried to catch up to
Peter. Zack faded into the crowd. At six-thirty on a summer evening it was still light enough to take pictures,
and he was making the most of the variety of faces and
types. Peter didn't seem to want to talk. He just drifted
about looking and listening. Rolf found some friends
and cadged a joint, and Wendy guessed that he sat
down with them to concentrate on more cosmic possibilities. She stood listening for a while and discovered
Peter had drifted out of her sight.

"I'll swap you a flower for a song."

It still surprised her that a stranger would speak to

her, and she jumped a little. Beside her stood a boy about her own age and height, his eyes dark, gentle and enormous. He was holding a large pink feather flower that was rather dirty and dilapidated around the edges.

"Oh, hi," said Wendy. "I just happen to be carrying this lute around with me. But I don't really like singing in a mob scene like this."

"You don't have to sing loud," he said. "Come on, sit down. Just play a little. Then maybe you'll feel like singing."

"Well—I'll sit down and talk anyway." There was an empty patch of grass near them, so they went and sat down.

He twirled the flower around and around in his fingers as if it were a Tibetan prayer wheel. "Do you come here often? I haven't seen you before."

"I just came yesterday. Do you really get to know people pretty well? I mean, are the same ones here all the time?"

"I know lots of faces. And some names. Sometimes I see them in Cambridge, and sometimes I see them here."

"Have you been here long?"

"I came to Cambridge last fall. But it's changed since summer began."

"How?"

"In the beginning it was just us. You know, real friends, true peace. We had love-ins on the Common, and it was real. It felt great, because we all felt the same way. A few people stood around and stared and wouldn't join in and made cracks. But now—well— there's us and there's them. And there's a lot more of them."

"Who's them?"

"You can tell. Look at those girls over there. They probably live in Newton or Brookline, and they spent three weeks' allowance on those ha-ha-hippie-ha-ha clothes at a boutique. I'll bet they don't even dare put

them on at home. They sneak somewhere to dress up.
See that guy? Bet he hung on his beads after he got off
the subway at Park Street. They're having a great time
pretending. But they're not real."

Is he going to spot me as real or unreal? Wendy wondered. *And which am I anyway? Jez and Rolf count me
as unreal, I'm sure. I wonder about this boy—*

"What's your name?" she asked.

"Donald. Donald Milner."

It seemed odd when he gave her a full name, and
she realized it was because everyone else she'd met,
except Peter, seemed to be identified by just one name—
Jez, Rolf, Oriana—even Zack. She still didn't know if he
was Zachary Something, or Someone Zacharias. She
found it touching that Donald should entrust her with
his whole name.

"I'm Wendy Allardyce."

They smiled at each other, and Wendy marveled
again at his eyes. He had fantastic long black eyelashes
and black curly hair. Donald was much more what
she'd expected to find—someone sweet and gentle and
honestly loving. Not crass, like Rolf. Or bossy, like Jez.
Or even cryptic, like Oriana or Peter. She began very
softly to play on her lute.

Across the street in the Public Garden, she saw again
the high, wide trees against a sunset sky. And this time
a little of the joy and excitement of an uncharted journey came back to her. Perhaps there was a sense of
peace and love that welled up in such a simple gathering of people who were all doing their own thing. All
she had to do was be awake to it.

She sang a short ballad, softly at first and then more
confidently as Donald gazed intently at her. A few people on the grass nearby turned their heads to listen and
several walking by stopped and waited till she finished.
It surprised her when a man with a red bolero over a
white open-necked shirt bowed politely and said,
"Thank you."

Donald handed her the flower.

"Thank you," said Wendy, and began to twirl it in her fingers. *What was it the Tibetans did with their prayer wheels anyway? Did every prayer cranked out mean a step up in the Everlasting?* She couldn't remember what she'd read. But the flower was almost hypnotic, and the buzzing and humming and mumbling and singing and discussing voices all around her could be that universal Om—not the frightening Om of the Mirabar Caves that terrified old Mrs. Moore. But the peaceful Om. Wendy looked around her and smiled benevolently, as if she, too, could bestow peace. It was an unexplainable, but very satisfactory, feeling.

"Are you happy?" asked Donald.

"Absolutely. I don't ever want to go back home. I wish this feeling would last forever. I wish the feeling in this moment would never change . . . that it would never grow old . . . never grow up!"

9

NEVER GROW UP! Wendy heard herself with horror. *A slip of the tongue,* she assured herself. *Not a Freudian slip of the mind.*

She sat up and shook herself, and the lute strings vibrated into sound.

"Is something the matter?" Donald asked.

"No! Not really. Unless you're one of the Lost Boys."

"Am I lost?" He was perplexed. Apparently Peter Pan allusions meant nothing to him. Wendy was relieved.

Donald went on, "My parents think I'm lost. But of course I'm not. There's been a note from them up on the runaway board for two weeks. I'll call home someday. Or send a message."

"Can't you let them know you're all right? You know —without giving in and going home or anything?"

"Perhaps. But it's such an abject note it embarrasses me. It says all kinds of forgive and forget things. But forgiving isn't free. It's a big clutch. I'd be worse off than I was."

Wendy, gazing again and again at his miraculous eyelashes and amazing eyes, could see why any mother of such a one would be frantic to locate him and would cry at night to wonder who might be kind or unkind to her beautiful child. *I'm going silly*, thought Wendy. *I'd better stop staring, like a bird about to gobble a worm, and sing a ballad.*

Just then a familiar-looking skirt swept into view. A girl knelt by Donald and threw her arms around him as if he were *her* long-lost child. "There you are! I've been looking everywhere for you. We're all set for the night, Donald. I've got everything you wanted."

It was Knocky Nell, and with a hurt in her heart, Wendy realized it was Donald that Nell had been begging for.

Donald reached out for the pink feather flower. "I only loaned it to you," he explained. "It's love-power comes from so many people holding it and loving it."

Surprised, Wendy let go of it. "Oh, of course. So I only loaned you the song."

"That's right." Donald's smile was so innocent.

If I wasn't right here in the midst of this, Wendy thought, *I'd wonder if he was simple or addled. Or simply addled. But that's being mean. He just has no pretenses. He's completely honest. And I wish Knocky Nell wasn't hanging all over him.*

Nell pulled Donald to his feet. "Come on. Everything's all fixed up."

Donald let her fuss, but he leaned down and stared into Wendy's face, as if he were searching for something. It gave Wendy an eerie feeling, but it made her feel alive and tingly, too.

"Will I see you around?" Donald asked.

"Absolutely!" Wendy jumped up. "You absolutely will." She said it as much to Nell as to Donald, and Nell led the boy briskly away.

"That's quite a pair." Peter materialized out of the crowd and stood by Wendy, watching Nell and Donald, arms around each other, retreat up the Common to the dimness of shade around the knoll.

"How come?"

"How come they paired up? She needed someone to mother, and he needed a mother, I guess. She can be rather a vulgar vulture, though. She swears she can tell which butt in the gutter is a roach and which isn't, without even bending to look close. She can tell which people to accost on the street and pick their conscience for a quarter. She has an instinct for fuzz. She could look around this area here and spot you five infiltrators right now."

"Infiltrators from what!" Wendy was shocked.

"Police. Feds. Salvation Army. Do-good church groups. Some out to get people. Some out trying to help."

"Why do people try to help people who don't want to be helped?"

"Why do you ask questions that are hard to answer?"

"All right. Answer one you can answer. How do you know all that about Nell? Have you been around here before?"

"Off and on. But Nell came to the Village last July. She was in a pad near me. She knows Oriana and Jez and Zack. Same people. Different locale, that's all."

"Donald wasn't around last summer, was he?"

"No. He's new."

"I don't think he's been away from home very long. What's the runaway board he was talking about?"

"It could be one of several. Salvation Army has one in their headquarters. The police have them in several precincts. There's two private organizations that post notices. You know, parents send pictures and ask has anyone seen this kid. Or they ask the kid to call home."

"Donald said his parents were looking for him." Wendy's voice trailed off. She couldn't help wondering what her family was doing about looking for her. She hadn't been away a full forty-eight hours yet. They had been revealing hours to her, which passed by easily because she was neither hoarding them nor spending them.

But what was happening at home? Was her father still hopefully phoning her friends? Had he phoned the police? Had her mother looked for her pictures and written letters? Had Ian claimed her room permanently? He hated being quartered with Dougal and always took over her room to sleep in when she was away. And Annetta would be delighted to pounce on her sweaters, while Rosalyn coveted most of her records. Would they really miss her as a person? *Maybe I'll send them a card,* thought Wendy. *Just so they won't worry. But they'll see the Boston postmark, and in two hours they'll be doing sentry duty on the Common. Maybe I'll direct dial on the phone and disguise my voice and ask for Dougal. He's so matter of fact I could just tell him to say I'm okay, and I'll see them again when I see them again. And he'd give the message without bothering to ask questions. After all, I wasn't really threatening to leave home quite this much.*

The decision that she might get in touch with them smoothed over the guilt she hadn't expected to feel and the uneasy moment passed.

Zack wandered up. "I haven't forgotten the sub I promised you. Hungry?"

"Starving! It's easy enough to ignore time by clocks and watches. But it's a lot harder to ignore it by stomach."

"Right." Zack clicked the case over his little camera. "The light's too far gone now anyway. Coming, Peter?"

"I'll join you," Peter said hastily. "At Gepetto's? I see a guy I've been looking for." He moved quickly away, and Wendy saw him catch up to the man in the red bolero jacket.

"Who's that?"

"He must be the guy Peter's been trying to contact."

"Why is he trying to contact someone? What is he doing anyway?"

"Still asking questions, aren't you!" Zack squinted at her, and she remembered his earlier remarks.

"Sorry. Just give me a sandwich. Something to eat will take my mind off anything else."

Gepetto's was a small basement room with two tiny tables and a counter. While Wendy was making up her mind, fascinated by all the combinations of ingredients chalked on a board, the man behind the counter greeted Zack with a big grin. "You gonna have a sub with all the fixings, you are. Linguisa and salami and bologna and pepperoni and all the best meaty cold cuts, a' right? You not going to have me fix you another one of those things don't deserve to be subs!" All the time he was whacking Swiss and cheddar and ricotta and mozzarella cheeses along with onions and red and green peppers and lettuce and relish and Italian dressing into the long, sliced roll.

"Here you are. You skinny. Should eat meat. Don't tell I make veg-e-tarian sub."

But Wendy could see he took pleasure in making it, even while he teased Zack. She ordered one with the works and dug into her jeans' pocket for change.

"Allow me," said Zack. "It's not often I take a girl out to dinner. Even if I have to invite her to eat standing up."

The tables were occupied, and when more people came in, Wendy and Zack barely had room left to stand in. But Peter didn't arrive before they finished. "Guess he got hung up," Zack said, and they wandered back up the Hill, detouring through Louisburg Square where Zack lingered, studying the houses even in the dusky light.

"This place fascinates me. It's so irrelevant that it's relevant."

"You meant it's so far out, it's in?"

"No. That's a status kind of statement. I'm agin that. It shouldn't matter where you come from or where you live status-tically speaking." He paused to let his horrible pun sink in, and Wendy groaned courteously.

"No. The kind of life this place represented in the past is so far removed from the mass of life today that it's irrelevant to us. But its irrelevance makes you reconsider its values. And that makes it relevant again. See?"

Wendy wasn't sure she did see, but she could feel the charming irrelevance settling restfully about her.

Back at Sage Lane, Zack took out his key and opened the door. Wendy wondered if he'd really needed the key. Apparently he wasn't aware of any trick to keep the door unlocked. The smell of curry penetrated all the way down to the second landing.

"Vivid, isn't it!" exclaimed Wendy.

"Come down if the smell gets you!" Zack told her.

When Wendy opened the door to the apartment, the sharp odor combined with the heat almost convinced her she was in India. Jez had changed from hot blue jeans to a psychedelically printed cotton shift, which was short enough to emphasize her stumpy legs. Wendy decided to change to her dress, as her jersey and jeans now felt like a sweat suit. She took her rucksack into the bathroom, stripped off her hot clothes, and plucked her wrinkled dress out of the jumble. There was a sudden banging on the door.

"Hurry up," Rolf's voice growled. "Emergency."

Wendy hastily wriggled into the dress and opened the door. Rolf did look uncomfortable, very white, and sweaty. He seemed faint.

"Can't get in the kitchen. Oriana's too busy." He grabbed at the cold-water faucet and turned it on full, trying to splash cold water over his face.

"Here, let me help." Wendy wrung a towel out in the cold water and wound it around his head and put a cold washcloth on the back of his neck. In a few minutes, his dizziness passed, and he went back to his

favorite spot, the hassock by the window. But he kept
the wet towel on like a turban.

Wendy then became aware for the first time of a tall
thin man who sat motionless on one of the couches. He
wore metal-rimmed round glasses. His sandy hair was
long, although not shoulder length. He wasn't really
ugly, but Wendy saw nothing particularly appealing
about his looks. Yet Jez and Oriana came from the
kitchen and sat on the floor, literally at his sandaled
feet, transfixed by his voice. He spoke in tones which
seemed carefully polished up from a rough Bronx ac-
cent, and he was apparently being fascinatingly profound. But his fascination to Wendy came because she
couldn't understand what he was saying enough to
figure out what he was talking about. But Oriana's
mind must have been trained along the same disciplines, because she occasionally asked just the right
question to draw out another involved answer from
William. Wendy was sure Jez, if she'd dared to relax,
would have unhinged her jaw and asked, "Huh?"

No one bothered to introduce Wendy. Oriana
acknowledged her presence with a queenly nod and
gave the impression it wasn't polite to interrupt William for a mere formality. His voice went on and on.
At first Wendy's curiosity kept her trying to tune in,
and she finally discovered that the earnest analysis concerned the basic principle of some obscure Buddhist
sect, but what it had to do with anything else, she
couldn't understand. It just grew very boring. She
knew what would happen at the dinner table at home
if anyone carried on in such a pompous manner. Everyone but her mother, who was too kind to join in, would
be sitting there planning traps and delighting in verbally tripping up the orator and bashing him when he
was down. But this was all so remote, Wendy couldn't
even think of a good trap. She almost nodded off to
sleep. It was fortunate that Zack had treated her to the

sub, because at midnight William was still talking and the curry was still simmering.

Then at some signal from William, Oriana, in a single movement as fluid as seaweed on the tide, floated to her feet. "Up, up, Jez!" she announced. "Up, Wendy! Come, Rolf. Our dinner is ready." She gave orders as demandingly as a head chef. A tablecloth was spread over the rug, and in moments they were all seated on the floor around plates and steaming dishes of rice and curry sauces.

Wendy had eaten curries before, so she was prepared for the throat-searing effect. Each mouthful seemed to light up the passages it traveled. *There ought to be a tape recording that goes along with each swallow,* Wendy thought, *saying "And now we are passing down through the esophagus, et cetera—"*

"This is all very illuminating," Wendy said, opening her mouth for a large swallow of cooling air.

"Oh, do you agree with my interpretation that the right views, the noble truths of the Eightfold Path should be reached by an intuitive grasp which can be attained much more quickly through drugs than through mental exercises?" asked William, apparently trying to give her a penetrating glance, but failing because his glasses were steamy.

Wendy hesitated. She had really been talking about the curry and its inside illumination. But she supposed she could play the dedicated disciple, too, and join Oriana and Jez in paying homage. The alternative did seem to be to play the dolt or the fool. But suddenly she remembered Dougal's favorite deflating trap, which was to throw in a red herring, an absolutely senseless question which unfortunately sounded sensible.

"Oh, no," said Wendy. "I don't agree. After all, don't you really feel that existentialism today is the mirror image of Nirvana?"

But sadly William had not waited for her answer. He

had already embarked in detail about another aspect of his theory. Oriana, however, swung a sharp look at Wendy.

Blast, thought Wendy. *She's the one who's pegged me as irreverent.* Wendy had hoped for Oriana's good opinion, and she could see that wasn't the way to get it.

Rolf, beside her, began gasping. He probably had eaten nothing since the grilled-cheese sandwich he'd swiped from Wendy earlier in the day, and he'd been gulping down the curry. Wendy thought he was going to faint again, and she grabbed the now-warm towel off his head. "I'll fix you another cold turban."

Rolf nodded, fanning his open mouth.

Oriana turned on him. "Rolf, where is your self-discipline? You're always suffering from some uncontrolled excess of something. One thing you should know, you cannot gobble curry."

"Who wants to be stuck with the concepts of discipline?" Rolf asked hoarsely. "Discipline just means acceptance of authority and conformity. And you know you don't go for that. That's your biggest preachment."

"Not anyone else's authority. Certainly not." Oriana's eyes flashed. "I'll challenge any law I feel is wrong. Like the grass laws! But I do have the integrity to impose disciplines on myself."

"You mean you're the only one who has the right to say what you will or won't do." Jez proudly interpreted Oriana's statement. "No one else has the right to tell you what to do."

"Of course. That's only sensible."

Wendy flapped the cold towel around Rolf's head, letting some of the water dribble down his neck. He shivered gratefully.

William ate steadily. Oriana ran a finger around one of the serving dishes and licked it with much satisfaction. But when the door opened and Charlene and Robbie came in, she urged them to join the feast and went to cook more rice. Within an hour there wasn't a bit of food left, except for half a box of raisins.

It was impossible to move in the kitchen without knocking over a pile of dirty dishes so Wendy made a start at washing up. But when no one bothered to help her, she quit. The others sprawled around, on floor or couches, and all were smoking. When Rolf handed Wendy a joint he'd just rolled, she decided she might as well join them and sat on the floor beside him. *Help stamp out dish-washing*, she thought, as she took a puff. *Help stamp out fuss.* She smoked slowly and dreamily and before too long she felt as if every muscle in her body had stretched with one little *ping* and then gone limp. Rolf handed her another—and later, another.

Oriana put on a Ravi Shankar record, and the tweaks and twangs, ripples and drones of the sitar as the *raga* went on and on vibrated in Wendy's mind. Thousands of notes tumbled quickly into the air, but she was sure each one trembled with color. She concentrated on this for a long time. When the music stopped, Wendy felt jolted back into the company of people. She stared at them, because their faces all seemed to open out like flowers, and the necks were all long, like stems, thin and white. The heads bobbed at her, atop their stems. Words kept falling on them, like nourishing showers of rain, as the talk went on and on and ever on. William for once was listening to Oriana, who was describing some moment of revelation that had come to her after a double dose of downers and meditation.

"Pardon me," Wendy was surprised to hear her voice come out so loudly. She had expected it to be more the buzz of a bee or the rasp of a branch in the wind. But it was unexpectedly real, and she felt she was holding her voice in her hands, as if it were a rope. "But Oriana, I thought all the Eastern religions scorned drugs. How do you reconcile pot and goof balls and being a Buddhist or a goddess or whatever it is you say you are?"

"Didn't you understand William's explanation of

why we don't accept the plain Buddhist theories? You
must relax and free your mind completely before you
can meditate successfully. Some religions do it just by
physical and mental disciplines—like Yoga and Zen
Buddhism. But it's just as successful and a lot quicker
to relax and free your mind with pot or LSD or peyote
or mescaline. After all, the Indians combined their
religion with the use of peyote."

"Ummm," said Wendy. Suddenly pages of the reading she'd done for Comparative Religion floated into
her mind. Words and names danced in front of her, in
all kinds of exotic scripts. She saw a shelf of bottled
words, labeled like jars in a drugstore, and she could
pick them up and shake them as needed. She heard
herself talking and talking, and it seemed to make
much more sense than she usually made. *Zap!* she
thought, *if only I'd filled up a blue book at the exam
with this discussion, I'd have made an A-plus-plus.*

"But why do you think that?" someone asked, and
she saw Peter's head standing stiffly on a wiry neck. He
crawled over and sat next to her.

Ordinarily she would have stuttered or stammered,
scratching around hopefully for a fact in her messy
mind. But again the words poured out. What a lovely
feeling of rapport it gave her and of authority, as the
flower-heads on the stems nodded and bowed and
listened and listened. *I'm pretty profound,* Wendy told
herself happily. *And I'd never, never have found all
this out about me if I'd gone on sitting at home and
listening to all that inhibited dinner-table chat.*

Then William took over and began expounding
again. This time Wendy felt every word was a gem of
meaning. Rolf was right about the cosmic experience
of it all—whether it was visual or aural, it certainly
awakened unused parts of her mind. Light struck off
William's steel-rimmed glasses, flashing out in long
bright rays that went from white intensity through all
the colors of the rainbow. Someone put an arm around

her and pulled her back against a broad shoulder. She put her head back to rest against the warm, solid, slow-breathing body, but her eyes now watched the lights splashing on the ceiling. There were occasional flashes as brilliant as summer lightning, and then as she blinked, the rainbow drops would shimmer off her eyelashes and fall into her eyes like strings of glowing beads. Her eyes stung, but she kept staring at the colors and the patterns in the colors. She saw beautiful complicated landscapes inside colored balloons. After a while a tremendous fog swept in and stuffed her ears and then her eyes and even her nose. But she was too tired to protest. She sank into it, and very vaguely and far away she heard someone saying, "I'm sure she's out like a light. Probably won't wake up until noontime." The body propping her up slid away, and she fell down through the fog onto a sandy beach, where she lay listening to the roar of the sea in her own ears.

That was the last thing she remembered until she woke up the next day. She was flat on the floor, and the dirty rug left an imprint on her face. She pushed herself up onto her knees. She felt limp, but her mind was clear. She saw William and Oriana sharing a couch near the kitchen, and Charlene and Robbie the other. Apparently she and Rolf and Jez had all spent the night on the floor. She could see Jez now, however, in the kitchen, and Rolf was already on the hassock by the window, smoking. It was raining out, and he had the window wide open, enjoying the cool sound as well as the damp wind. There was no sign that Peter had ever been there, although she was sure he had.

Her mouth was dry. She joined Jez and put the kettle on for tea. She looked at the heaps of dirty dishes left from the feast and made a face of disgust. "We certainly ate enough last night. I shouldn't feel hungry, but I do."

Jez held out the half box of raisins. "Have some. And there's still some tea bags if you want tea."

Wendy nodded and munched on some raisins. She drank the tea gustily and made herself a second cup. Jez had been exploring several sugar bowls and cream pitchers and found a quarter in one, but that was all. She looked at it thoughtfully apparently wishing it would start to grow in her hand.

"Wendy—" Jez spoke quietly. "Did you have a good time last night?"

"Yes, I did," Wendy admitted. "And I feel just fine this morning. I honestly don't see why all the rot about pot. What I saw with my very own eyes was certainly a lot more fascinating than any TV program and more than most movies. Why do people get so up-tight about it?"

"Some people get up-tight because it's pot. But some people just get up-tight if anyone does anything he's been told not to do. They'd fly into a rage if they said don't put beans up your nose and you put beans up your nose. There are just some people who always feel they have to be obeyed, no matter if they're right or wrong."

"That's true," said Wendy. "Like parents." She started on her second cup of tea, but drank it more slowly.

"Would you do us a favor?" Jez asked.

"What?"

"In that suitcase there are some old things I want to sell."

"I don't really need anything—" Wendy began.

"I don't mean sell to you! I mean sell to a secondhand shop."

"Then why don't you? There are plenty of shops around here."

"I've already disposed of several boxes of things," Jez said hastily. "Things I had shipped up when I came. They belonged to my great-aunt. Before she died. In New Jersey. I was going to help Oriana furnish the place with them. But who wants a lot of useless lamps and clocks and silver stuff that has to be polished? The trouble is that I've taken stuff to all the shops around here, and they know I'm—well, just no good at bargaining. So they take advantage of me. I don't get my money's worth."

Wendy could hardly believe that. She felt Jez was aggressive enough to fight for the last penny. But perhaps Jez had lost an advantage, if she'd been a fairly regular seller.

"You bought last night's supper, right?" Jez reminded her. "Oriana and William are clean out of funds. She told me. Rolf doesn't have any right now. Charlene and Robbie come and go. They're apt to come empty-handed and go when they find something, though. And it's my turn to provide. So I need to sell something out of the suitcase. All you have to do is go into that shop— the one where you looked at the earrings—and take what he'll give you for it."

"If you're poor at bargaining, I can promise you, I'm worse." Wendy didn't want to do it. But Jez had already dragged out the case. She finally picked out a clock and handed it to Wendy. "Please take it and see what you can do. I want to buy some coffee and eggs before Oriana and William get up. It's for everyone's good you know. Not just me."

Reluctantly Wendy took the clock.

10

"Going for a walk?" Rolf watched Wendy scrabbling about in her knapsack for her raincoat. He stood up and stretched. He gave her the impression of being a great balloon with a slow leak.

"Want to come?" Wendy asked eagerly. She didn't want to take the clock into the store by herself.

"Rolf better stay here," Jez insisted. "If old Mr. Volmarr sees you're with Rolf, he'll knock the price right down. But with that dress on, Wendy, and that raincoat, he surely won't think of you as a hippie. You'll do better that way."

"How much is the clock worth?" It was about ten inches high with a brass-and-glass case, and Wendy could see all its parts working away earnestly inside.

"Haven't the vaguest," said Jez.

Slowly Wendy drew on her coat.

"Good morning!" Oriana was awake. She sat up and made stretching into a ballerina's exercise—her arms and neck without an ugly angle, her hands curved gracefully. "Another be-jeezly day, is it?" Oriana drifted to the window, the rumpled purple tunic making her look even more like a delicate spring flower emerging from a bulb's dark winter sheath. *Like one of the snowdrops by the house,* thought Wendy. Even Oriana's white cheek seemed to have a snowdrop kind of curve.

"Rain! A day to be spent happily within!" Oriana turned contentedly away from the window. "What do we need, Jez, for a quiet day at home?"

"Everything. I'm sending Wendy out with a clock to see Mr. Volmarr."

"Jez! You are reliable. What would we do without you, William and I? Well, go on, Wendy. We really are all just plain broke."

"All right. I'm off. But give me a paper bag to put this in. I feel crass carrying it naked through the streets. At least it doesn't tick as loud as a bomb."

All was quiet behind Zack's door as she passed the second-floor landing. Again she wondered what Peter's game was. At first when he talked about contacts and looking for people and going back to his old life, she thought he might be trying to find a pusher, settling down to one who knew him and to one he trusted to sell him good grade. He'd even joked about finding a Captain Hooked. But Wendy realized he seemed to be very busy. He didn't lie around, dreaming off the hours the way Rolf did. If Rolf were a typical consumer, Peter was not. Wendy wasn't sure if Peter had been smoking pot last night even though he'd been there with them.

Maybe he was a pusher, and that was why he was always rushing busily off somewhere. But Wendy didn't like that thought. It was much more comfortable to go along with the separate steps of this thing than admit the whole scene—like eating a nice steak without picturing the slaughterhouse. She enjoyed a joint, but she didn't particularly want to know all the processes by which it reached her hand. The thought of Peter pushing was as shocking to her as seeing Knocky Nell panhandle.

But I'm making judgments again, she reminded herself, as the rain splashed down her neck. *And who am*

*I to say what's right or wrong? Especially where other
people are concerned.*

She turned up her coat collar. Somehow while rain
felt refreshing in her hair and delicious on her bare
toes, it was an indignity down her neck.

She remembered Oriana, somewhere in the welter of
last night's words, saying firmly that the laws about
possessing pot or even being found in the presence of
pot were all wrong—and if she, Oriana, were arrested,
she didn't mind. Because it would take honest and
brave people like herself to fight unjust laws like that.
The same, she said, as laws about not giving out birth-
control information were wrong. She did not intend to
have any children for a long time. She didn't intend to
marry for a long time, either, although she and William
had worked out a compatible relationship. But mar-
riage would spoil it. Children would spoil it. Oriana's
reason for her way of life had been repeated often
enough to stick in Wendy's mind like a refrain: *How
can I understand myself as a person, how can I find the
real inside me, the gem of myself, if I have to share
myself through artificial and arbitrary relationships?*

Wendy remembered saying she could see how mar-
riage could be considered an arbitrary relationship, but
she doubted a child could. "What's artificial about a
mother-and-child relationship?" she wanted to know.
"That's about as physical as you can get."

"I'm not talking about physical aspects," argued
Oriana. "There's chemical control of all kinds of physical aspects today, and people should use it. I'm talking
about moral blackmail. That's how children and families usually turn out."

"I don't agree!" Wendy was gleefully horrified. She
thought of herself and Rosalyn, Annetta, Dougal and
Ian lined up, as at a fire drill, for the moral blackmail
of her parents and burst out laughing. "Oriana! You
can't be serious!"

But Oriana, her face grim and her teeth gritted, said,

"Who needs kids! Not until I'm an old and wise woman would I dare have one. And then I'm not sure I'd really want one."

How sad, thought Wendy. *Something's so sad about her.* She'd wanted to ask all kinds of questions about Oriana's childhood. Nobody's childhood was perfect, but could hers have been all that bad? But Oriana refused to be drawn into a personal conversation and argued furiously about abstractions and theories with Robbie and William. It had shaken Wendy a bit, pondering Oriana's exquisite beauty and wondering what was real inside. But perhaps that sad awareness had also been a product of the pot she was smoking then. For this morning's Oriana, calm and serenely graceful, bore no resemblance to the grim girl suddenly revealed last night.

What a confusion life is if you try to understand it! Wendy thought. *It's far better to stop worrying about life and just live it as it comes.* She began to look around her again and tried to stop feeling apprehensive about her errand. *It's just a part of my new life,* she assured herself.

She strode down the steps to the shop and looked around it in delight. She saw the earrings at once and couldn't help asking, "How much are they? Those earrings in the window? The silver ones with the dark-red stones."

A polite old man, neatly dressed and quite knowledgeable about the difference between the merely secondhand and the genuine antiques, smiled at her eagerness.

"I probably can't afford them if they're old. But I'd like to know anyway."

The man reached into the window. Wendy put her paper bag down on a glass-topped case full of old silver sugar tongs and odd-shaped serving spoons. "They are quite old. Probably a hundred years. Those are garnets. A favorite stone with New England ladies who wanted a little color, a little sparkle, but didn't want to spend a lot of money."

"Do you mind?" Wendy picked one up and swished back her glistening wet hair. She saw a handsomely framed mirror and stood before it, holding up the earring. The three little silver pendants, each swinging a small, brightly faceted garnet, looked charming.

"How much?" Wendy, having nothing like it in her collection, was terribly tempted.

"Twelve dollars plus tax."

"Oh." Wendy knew she should tell him to put them right back in the window. She had already spent about half the money she'd started with. And once her cash went, that was it!

"It's genuine antique jewelry," said the man encouragingly.

"I know, I know. But my problem is I just shouldn't spend money for earrings." She remembered the clock, and a stab of chagrin shot through her stomach. "As a matter of fact, I came in to see if you'd be interested in buying this clock."

His expression stiffened. But Wendy looked so embarrassed that he tried to smile politely as she handed him the clock. "This is nothing antique, you know," he said. "Common garden variety eight-day windup clock made in Germany. Although it is old enough to have been made in Old Germany, not so-called West or East Germany. Maybe even made in my hometown." He sighted off through his rimless glasses at a distant past. Apparently it was a happy past, as he really smiled this time.

Wendy smiled, too. "I know it's only a secondhand kind of thing, but it looks awfully well made. I'm sure it keeps wonderful time."

"Don't you know? Isn't this yours? I've had too much of kids coming in here to sell me things. I mistrust how they come by them, but I can only take their word."

"Well, a friend did give it to me. But I don't need

another clock. I'm used to an electric one. I'd never remember to wind this."

"Bah! Everyone's getting too lazy to wind clocks, even. Except after the big power blackout." He chuckled. "I sold out all my windup clocks in two days." He picked up the clock again. "Must say it's in excellent condition. Could have been made by my father."

"Where?"

"In Stuttgart. Yes, that's just the kind my father and his father before him worked on in the factory. You're sure you don't want to keep this? They don't make clocks as good as this any more."

"No. No. I don't need it."

"I can only give you fifteen dollars for it."

"That's all right." Wendy smiled. Fifteen dollars sounded large, as if it could buy a week's groceries unless Oriana went in nightly for exotic curries.

"I'll give you sixteen for it if you want to buy the earrings." The man saw she still looked at them longingly.

"I can't!" Wendy said it fast, so she wouldn't give in. But then she remembered Jez had a suitcase full of things, and it might be easier to sell another item to this man now, if she had such an obvious excuse. "Well—maybe I have something else you could buy. If you bought something else, then I could afford to spend the extra for the earrings. I'll be back."

She ran out, leaving the clock and without waiting for the money. What she was doing didn't really make sense, but she was impulsive and excited about it. By the time she'd hiked rapidly up the hill and two flights of stairs, she was breathless. Coming into the apartment was like bursting in on a game of Still Pond No More Moving. Everyone seemed exactly where she'd left them—Rolf on the hassock, Charlene and Robbie and William asleep. Jez and Oriana sitting on the floor talking.

"Jez! Do you want me to sell something else now?

I've sort of got a trade going, I think. You do want to get rid of all that stuff, don't you?"

Jez was amazed. "I wasn't even sure you'd manage to sell the clock! How much will he give you for it?"

"Maybe sixteen. Is that all right?"

"It's more than he'd have given me. Take a look in the suitcase. See what you think he'd go for."

She dragged it out and Wendy wondered just what kind of a woman Jez's great aunt had been. There was a tarnished silver-backed mirror with a "W" engraved into the design, some mother-of-pearl opera glasses, a tortoise-shell lorgnette, a silver-beaded drawstring bag, a modern toaster, three pairs of silver candle-sticks, and a pair of brass ones. There were some thin, coin silver spoons that Wendy knew were quite old and some rather large binoculars in a worn leather case.

"Let me take the binoculars. And the opera glasses. I think those are funny."

"Don't let him gyp you on the binoculars," Rolf warned. "Those are expensive. You ought to get at least thirty dollars out of him."

"But don't fuss," Jez ordered. "Take what you can get. Don't you think she should just take what she can get, Oriana?"

"By all means."

Wendy hurried back, but the man sighed when he saw the binoculars. "I really thought maybe you were different. Especially when you ran off and left the clock without grabbing your money."

"But I came back because I want the earrings. Remember? I don't care about those heavy binoculars. I don't bird-watch. I'll never use them, so why keep them? But I love those little opera glasses. Aren't they pretty?"

He still looked at her sadly, shaking his head. "Don't you want to keep them if they're pretty?"

"But I don't go to the opera."

"Who does any more? Even in Boston." Then he became businesslike, sharp and hard. "I said sixteen for the clock, against twelve and tax for the earrings. I'll only give you two dollars for the pretty opera glasses and fifteen for the binoculars."

"Is that all? Aren't the binoculars good ones?"

"They are indeed. But that's all I'll give you for them," he scowled at her and then went on bitterly, "I hoped you were different."

Wendy didn't know whether to cry or stamp her foot. "What's so terrible about selling old things I don't need? When I want to buy some earrings and some groceries? Do you always make a personal kind of lecture out of buying things? Isn't buying things your business, too?"

"I'm sorry," said the man. "I'm upset today. You see— I'm trying to make up my mind whether to sell my business or not. For twenty-five years I've been right in this spot. I've enjoyed it. Twenty-five years of meeting people and making them happy to find something they've wanted. Like your earrings. And even if I'm not a Yankee, I've enjoyed the bargaining. It's been satisfying. But it's all changed. I don't want any part of it any more. Young people come in with their childish faces and babyish bodies and their hard, hard eyes and tough tongues. They come to sell and hardly anyone comes to buy. I'm frightened how they spend their money and spend their lives. I've been robbed three times. No, it's all changed. There's no fun and no joy. It's all grim."

"Will you go somewhere else?"

"My kind of trade? My kind of store? There's not many places I could go. And the troubles in the cities are all the same. Nowadays there isn't any 'somewhere else.' " He stood looking at her sorrowfully.

"That's too bad. I'm sorry about selling the things. But you did make me happy about the earrings. I'll put them on."

While he counted out the money, she slipped out the

small gold studs she was wearing and set in the garnets, twinkling on their silver threads.

"Enjoy them," he said. "What's going on around here now is all supposed to be joy—joy and freedom and love. I see the freedom. The love may be there, the way couples hang all over each other. But the joy I don't see. And don't let me catch you out on that sidewalk looking for dope. If you were my little girl, I'd spank you. I really would spank you."

He turned his back on her and went to fuss with some things on a shelf. Wendy could see he was too upset to go on talking. All she could do was stop before she shut the door against the rain and call back to him, "Well, thanks for letting me buy the earrings anyway."

But his sadness and helplessness kind of spread over her, and she frowned as she walked along. She could see where the shopkeepers might be concerned because the influx of hippies would upset their balance of trade. But that man surely was too sensitive, taking it all too personally. *Must be kind of a nut,* Wendy decided. *But a nice nut.*

Anyway, there'd be some joy when she handed Jez the twenty dollars and sixty-four cents cash she'd realized on the transaction. And an I.O.U. for twelve dollars and thirty-six cents on the earrings. Only then did she realize that where she and her sisters operated on a complicated system of I.O.U.'s against their allowances, Jez might not. Also, just how did Wendy expect her allowance to reach her when she'd removed herself from the family circle? Since she'd never had to provide for herself, Wendy hadn't really yet faced one solid economic fact of life—no parents, no job, no money.

Jez was pleased with the cash. She put it in the sugar bowl in the kitchen. She was not pleased with the I.O.U.

"If we used a system like that around here, we'd starve. No, you up with the cash if you've got it."

Oriana added, "The things to sell were donated by

Jez, so you have no right to divert the money they raised. It isn't ethical."

Wendy gave up and agreed with them. She had been rash to splurge on something she wanted but didn't need, and she could only face the consequences. But she was confused by Oriana's insistence that her using the money, even if she offered an I.O.U., wasn't ethical. Just last night Oriana had been denouncing federal laws about narcotics and state laws about birth control and saying she was perfectly willing to flout them and challenge them because they weren't ethical. Breaking a law still seemed more unethical to Wendy than using money she certainly intended to repay. There was a twist to either her mind or Oriana's mind that was going to take some sorting out.

She felt around in her knapsack and decided now was the time to get rid of the rest of Dougal's change. So she had to dump everything out on the floor and take a good look at the total contents. Once she paid Jez twelve dollars and thirty-six cents she certainly didn't have very much left! She remembered the gold-stud earrings in her raincoat pocket and picked up the painted wooden box containing her earring collection. Even though she slid the studs in quickly, she thought Jez gave the box a calculating glance.

Peter popped his head in at the door. "Wendy, I'm going away. Back tomorrow night. Just thought I'd tell you so you could miss me."

"Where?"

"New York. Want to come?"

"No. I like it fine right here."

"If you're all set, I'll dash."

"Wait a minute, Peter. You could do me a favor. You could mail a postcard for me from New York. If I had a postcard to write on."

"Zack may. Come down."

Zack didn't, but they improvised one out of cardboard and found a stamp. Wendy addressed it to "The

Allardyces, Meridian Farm, RFD, Westerly, R.I." Then her mind felt blanker than the card.

"You don't have to write it in sonnet form," Peter said impatiently. "Just say it."

"Saying 'say it' is easier than saying it," Wendy muttered. Finally she wrote: "Everything OK. Having a great time and finding the real me. DON'T WORRY. I can cope. Love, Wendy."

Peter stood right in front of her and read every word. Then he nodded and stuck it in his pocket.

"I trust you approve!" Wendy said indignantly.

"Very well said, as a matter of fact. If you get into difficulties, Zack will be in and out." Peter steered her out, set the latch, and locked the door. He carried his beat-up zipper bag. "Now be a good girl and miss me."

"Why do you tell me to be a good girl? What business is it of yours?"

"I suddenly feel older-brotherly and responsible now I'm going off and leaving you."

"I never particularly wanted an older brother."

"When I come back, I'll remember that." He kissed her goodby, and halfway down the stairs, turned around and said again, "Take care now."

Wendy laughed at him. "I fail to see what is so devastating or dangerous about how I'm living. So far it's been nothing but a lot of talk and some smoke."

Peter grinned and dashed out the door. Wendy found Jez coming downstairs, wearing Wendy's raincoat. "Hope you don't mind. I'm going out to buy groceries. Oriana made another list."

This time Wendy found William and Charlene and Robbie were all awake and Jez had been sent scurrying to buy instant coffee, among other things. No one was doing much talking. Wendy put her rucksack under her head and lay on the floor, reading *To Call It Sleep*. When she finished it in the afternoon, she looked around for her coat, as it had suddenly become communal property. Even Oriana had borrowed it when she ran out on an errand and had left it sogged in a heap in a corner.

Wendy began to realize why the apartment felt so transient. Aside from her lute and Oriana's poster and a few records, there were no personal belongings strewn about. She was used to living in a helter-skelter of things—in a real mess at school. Even at home, books and magazines drifted in a perpetual high tide around the house, with her mother's half-finished craft projects marooned on little tables, abandoned until she was swept back again with time to work on them. Once a weaving project in a table loom sat unfinished for so long that her father referred to it as a piece of permanent household sculpture entitled "Mother's Unwoofed Warp." Wendy herself enjoyed picking up something to do with her hands, and without some knitting or sewing or painting, she felt lost. Restlessly she went out to find some more paperbacks to read, and when she came back, she was still restless. So she took out her lute and played and sang softly to herself for an hour or so.

After she finished a long involved English ballad, Robbie asked, "Do you know Arlo Guthrie's 'Alice's Restaurant?' "

"I wish I did. But it's so long he's the only one who knows it. It's funnier than lots of old ballads."

"It's sadder, you mean."

"Now that is where the concept of humor arises," William began. "The conflict of tragedy and comedy produce humor." He was off with such earnestness that he took all the fun out of the argument, although Robbie seemed to enjoy needling him and kept the discussion going until Wendy lost interest completely.

It was still raining out when it grew dark. Rolf quietly went to the kitchen, fished in the sugar bowl, took out some money, tossed Wendy's raincoat over his shoulders and departed.

Oriana, Jez, and Wendy all bumped into each other in the kitchen, making a spaghetti sauce. But people ate whenever they were in the mood. Rolf returned eventually with enough grass for a few joints and the night rolled on into a rerun of the night before.

As did the next day and the next night. But the day after that the rain stopped, and the sidewalks and the houses and the people in the attics and the basements all steamed. They wandered over to the Common the day the sun came out, and Wendy found herself looking especially for Donald. She was tired, whether from lack of sleep at some times and too much sleep at others or the irregular food or the being hunched up in close quarters continually with other people, she didn't know. She just knew her eyes felt grainy and tired, and her head ached.

She went down to the Common long before anyone else in the apartment and climbed the little knoll by the silly monument and lay under the shade of a tree labeled *Ulmus Americanus. Boston would name its trees so everyone will get educated,* she thought sleepily. She wondered if the city officials were printing up little cards to pin on the people who were trying to be as indigenous to the Common—maybe *Hippus Hoppedus,* or some such words would occur to them. It was a wonder they didn't make the pigeons carry ID's. *What if an Uncommon Pigeon infiltrated the Common Pigeons?*

There was an aggregation of pigeons now, down by the bandstand. Two old men sat on opposite benches, enjoying their afternoon fun of feeding the birds, and several hundred pigeons squabbled about on the sidewalk. Suddenly a girl on the knoll near Wendy hopped up. She wore bell-bottoms, but a green satin pseudo-Russian blouse hung over them to her thighs. She trailed a long pink chiffon scarf over her shoulder and around her arms, the ends making wings behind her. A straw hat, with flowers clustered around the large brim, shaded her head. She yelled "Who-eeee!" and came flapping down on the birds.

The pigeons took off in a turmoil, making people throw their arms protectively over their heads. Feathers and droppings flew about as the birds circled in a squawking cloud. The girl still dashed about, waving her pink scarf and calling "Who-eee! Who-eee!"

One of the men walked over to her. "What did you want to go and do that for? You got everything all stirred up now! I thought you crumbs was all for peace and brotherhood. Look at the fuss you made."

The man grew very upset and red in the face.

The girl turned her face in his direction, but it was obvious she didn't really hear him. She kept waving the pink scarf and dancing in and out among the pigeons. "Sing 'who-ee' and dance, dance with the pigeons!" The man grabbed at her arm. At the same time, Wendy saw a slender boy run up and grab her other arm.

"Come over here, Nell. The pigeons are busy. Come dance over here."

She took his hand, and they ran gaily up the slope and fell down laughing on the grass near Wendy.

"It was so beautiful," gasped Nell. "All that whirring of wings and the arcs the wings made in the sunlight. There was the most fantastic feeling of flying in the air. I had wings, too, Donald. Just try it!"

She gave him the pink scarf, but instead of chasing pigeons with it, he tied it round and round his waist. "Lie down, Nell," he said, "and I'll read to you." He pulled a battered foreign paperback from his pocket and began reading poetry in French. Looking up to turn a page, he saw Wendy and recognized her with a welcoming smile. Without a word, Wendy moved over and lay down close by him on the grass.

"I don't know French," Nell said happily, lying with her eyes closed, "but I can understand every word you say, Donald."

Donald read on with an ease that made Wendy wonder where he'd learned his French. It was like listening to music, and again Wendy had such an acute feeling of peace and happiness. How simple her life became with no commitments and no pressures, with time to enjoy. *I've stopped feeling up-tight at last,* Wendy discovered. *How can my parents possibly disapprove of this kind of life, when it's so full of peace and happiness and culture, even! Too bad they're stuck with their stuffy, stuffy world.*

When Rolf came along and found her, he sat down, gave her a few puffs of his rolled cigarette and pulled her back to rest against him. At first she'd hated any touch from Rolf. There was something coarse and pasty about him that made her uncomfortable. Besides she had only to look at Donald to feel as if she were melting. If Donald so much as touched her, she knew she'd follow him anywhere. But Rolf had become a constant companion, especially with Peter away, and she couldn't spend all her time shaking him off and saying, "Down, boy!" as if he were O'Casey, the setter. So she resigned herself to his being around, without either fighting him or encouraging him.

Donald closed the book. Nell lay asleep. The reading had been a perfect lullaby. "Wendy," Donald said, reaching for her hand, "come take a walk with me. I want to talk with you."

Rolf, gripping her shoulder, kept her from getting up. "It's too hot to walk. You can talk just as well right here. Without moving."

"No," said Donald. "The best basis for understanding is a one-to-one relationship. Not two-to-two." He nodded at Nell. "Wendy and I need to understand each other."

"We'll be back," Wendy promised, moving quickly enough to slide out from under Rolf's grip. "After all, that's what I'm here for. More understanding!"

Wendy knew Rolf stared at them as she and Donald strolled off hand in hand. She even heard him say, "What you'd better make sure is that Nell understands."

11

AFTERWARD WENDY THOUGHT of the walk with Donald as a kind of *Pilgrim's Progress,* because it had so many phases. She wasn't conscious of time as hour of the day or night. She didn't worry any more about the right time for eating or sleeping, because both could be accomplished in odd moments. But later, when Peter made her think about her walk with Donald, she finally admitted that the journey must have taken most of forty-eight hours, even though it seemed to flow from one spontaneous event to another.

From the Common, they wandered to the Public Garden, and Donald thoroughly enjoyed a ride with Wendy on the Swan Boat. When she found she had several dollars in change, they went around a second time while Donald recited the story of "The Ugly Duckling." He insisted on telling it to the acne-faced boy pedaling the boat. "Don't be discouraged," Donald begged him. "Keep pedaling and be kind to the ducks and at the end of the summer, you, too, will be a swan."

The boy swore at him.

Donald and Wendy meandered through the streets until they came to Chinatown. "Do you want some supper?" Wendy asked, wondering how far her money would go, but tempted by her love of Chinese food.

"Let's not eat indoors. Let's buy something we can eat by the river. Maybe there's a concert tonight."

So they changed their direction and passing a small grocery bought bread and bologna and two cans of Sprite. Donald clutched the paper bag as they walked through a run-down neighborhood. He pointed across the street to where an attempt had been made to paint up and cheer up an old store. An assortment of abandoned easy chairs were placed inside—some isolated, some arranged as for consultation. Kids of various ages sat tensely in them or slept easily. At the back of the room were two tables with telephones, and several older men sat there, talking with kids. The side walls of the room seemed to be hung with papers, letters, notes, and pictures. A cardboard sign in the front window read: "HELP HAVEN, Inc. Try us—we make connections."

"There's a letter from my parents in there," Donald announced. "Whenever I think maybe I might like to go home, I stop by and read it. Then I don't care again. Tonight I feel very free of that letter." He smiled at Wendy. "I'll just go on letting it hang there. Just believe me. I know what I'm talking about." He seemed very emphatic and excited, almost as if he were convincing himself of how he ought to feel.

Wendy, although she'd had a puff or two on the joint Rolf was smoking, didn't feel high at all. But when Donald put his arm around her and steered her around the corner, she felt high on just plain emotion in a very physical sense. *If this is what just a touch will do,* Wendy thought, *what's going to happen when he kisses me? I'll be absolutely gone.*

They didn't talk. After all the words and theories and discussions and more words she'd heard from Peter and Zack and Rolf and William and Robbie, Donald's si-

lence was like balm. His invitation to talk and then his
refusal just to chatter about inconsequentials or to nat-
ter a theory to death made her feel far closer to him
than an exposé of his life history.

When they reached the bank of the Charles, they sat
on the grass and ate the bread and bologna, and drank
the Sprite. Across the wide, gray-colored water was the
squat dome of an M.I.T. building, burned pink like a
bald head in the sunset. Old and new buildings stacked
their odd shapes against the sky. Small sailboats still
drifted along the river where streaks of sunset red
bounced back dirtily at the sky. When Wendy went to
the edge and took off her sandals, Donald warned her.
"I have heard it told, as a very reliable folk rumor, that
your toes will get polluted and drop off if you stick your
feet in the Charles."

A motor launch passing by churned the muddy
water, and it looked thick, as if it had a crust. Wendy
didn't put her feet in, much as she wanted to cool them.
She sat there, smelling the stale wetness of the water
and wondering if the tide were high in the Wallow and
if by any chance Annetta and Rosalyn had beaten the
little boys down for a swim and taking possession of the
spot, shucked their suits for a last cooling dip of the
day.

"You're not feeling lonely, are you, Wendy?"

"How could you tell?"

"People feel lonely when their faces go far away. You
know when you're talking to someone, and you discover he's looking at you, but he's not listening. That's
how you are now."

"But I'm right here with you. All alone with you."

The sense of isolation didn't last. Couples and families strolled by as an enormous crowd gathered farther
down the river for the Esplanade Concert. Wendy and
Donald drifted along, too, sitting on the grass at the
outskirts of the crowd. The Boston Pops Orchestra
played from the shelter of a concrete acoustical shell,

mixing light classical pieces with marvelous arrangements of show tunes and pop music. Singable, hum-
mable, whistleable, danceable music. It all went with
Wendy's airy, giddy mood, and she could hardly sit
still. But Donald's sweet touch made her feel even more
airborne. Like the girl levitated in the magic act, Donald could levitate her with a look. Wendy had been in
and out of love before and been mad about a boy or
two. Yet this, unexpected and unexplained, shook her
as no previous encounter had.

After the dusk took over and the night sky deepened
to black, Donald sat with her in his arms and kissed her
slowly over and over again. She couldn't move. She
knew if she moved all the tiny tingling pieces she had
broken into would fall apart.

She didn't want to go back to Oriana's apartment and
share Donald with the group. Or worse yet, to find Rolf
glowering at her or Peter worrying about her and Nell
pouncing at Donald. So when the music ended and
Donald guided her along the riverbank, she didn't say
a word. Across the water the Carter's Ink sign neoned
its message, and under a layer of smoke and haze, the
glow of thousands of lights hung over the city like a
crooked and tarnished halo.

Donald seemed to know exactly where he was
headed, and he led her onto one of the bridges over the
Charles. The traffic made her wince as cars swooshed
past, and she had a feeling that pedestrians on the
bridge must have a death wish. She expected a police
whistle or a siren to stop them at any minute. Down the
middle were the tracks of the subway, temporarily
above ground and above river. The bridge had pairs
of little towers, built of granite blocks, at intervals, and
her aunt had called it the Salt and Pepper Bridge. Donald stopped at one of the towers and pulled her around
in back of it, where they could sit and look out over the
slowly swirling river. Aside from the zoom of cars and

occasional shrilling whoosh of the subway trains, it was
a tranquil spot.

"How did you ever find this place?" Wendy asked.

"Nell calls this her summer porch."

"Is Nell apt to come looking for you—on her porch?"

"Maybe."

"Then what?"

"We swim for it."

"In water that will rot off our toes!"

"Wendy, relax. Don't think up all the *if*'s all the time.
It ruins the *now*'s."

"You're right." Wendy gave up. They held each other
gently, and he talked and she talked, and time could
have been tucked away forever on a clock in the
stomach of the crocodile, and they wouldn't have
missed it. When at last the traffic had thinned and only
a few lonely planes climbed the skies with their burden
of travelers, Donald fell asleep. Wendy sat there, his
head on her shoulder. *This is one of those times I'll keep
packed away in my heart for always*, thought Wendy,
*but it won't stand unpacking and looking at. It might
disappear. I can't explain it, not even to me.*

When Donald woke, he had to help Wendy to stand,
as she felt as though her whole body had fallen asleep.
"Come on, we'll go over to Cambridge and see a friend
of mine." It was a relief to walk. Once off the bridge,
they hiked up river toward Cambridge, but Donald
turned off to the right before they came near any of the
Harvard buildings. He knew his route quite well and
without hesitation led to a basement apartment where
a brief knock on the door let him in.

"Just don't step on anyone who's fallen asleep,"
someone said, and although Wendy found it hard now
to lift her aching feet an inch higher than she had to,
she managed not to tread on anyone.

"If you're looking for the host, try the bedroom," a
girl said. "Last time I saw Charlie he was in there."

Wendy yawned. "Donald, where's the bathroom?

I've got to have a drink of water and maybe some aspirin."

He showed her the bathroom, and although she turned on a light, she didn't look at herself in the glass. *I'm not sure I know me*, she said groggily to herself. *And I must look terrible. I wish I could wash my hair.* It always bothered her if her hair felt the least bit dirty.

Although they opened the medicine cabinet, they couldn't see any aspirin. Donald went to find Charlie and ask if he had any. When he came back he had four pills in his hand. Wendy felt as if she were getting one of the tension headaches that sometimes incapacitated her at school for two days at a time. Sometimes she would overcome them by taking five aspirin at once and lying down for an hour with an icy-cold cloth over her eyes. So she automatically swallowed all four pills.

"Hey!" said Donald. "Two of those were for me!"

"I'm sorry. Do you have a headache, too? That was piggy of me, but four aspirin sometimes work where two don't."

"Those weren't aspirin. Charlie didn't have any."

"What—were—they!"

"You'll sure feel better fast. Speedily, as a matter of fact."

"You gave me some pep pills?"

"Right. Just a little speed can't hurt you, Wendy. Would I want anything to happen to you?" He bent toward her, and his huge dark eyes seemed to tip into hers. "Don't go panick-y over nothing. That's *so* nothing, I'm going to see Charlie about really speeding. Pills are too slow for me now anyway. Only shooting speed works for me any more."

He disappeared into the bedroom. Wendy sat on the edge of the tub, her feet still feeling like lead, but her heart pounding. A fine sweat popped out on her forehead and the palms of her hands. *That's silly,* she told herself. *Nothing could act that fast. I'm just scaring myself and being chicken.*

She went looking for Donald and squeezed into a space in the living room. The space kept changing its shape, as people around her danced with each other and danced by themselves. She danced, too. The beat of the music seemed to wind her up. Donald came and danced. He had always seemed so gentle that she was surprised by the wildness of his dancing. They danced through four whole records without stopping.

"I'm not even tired any more!" Wendy said. "I feel like the girl in the red shoes!"

"See? I told you speed was better than aspirin."

How long she danced she had no idea, but suddenly her knees gave, her back seemed to crumble, her arms went limp, and she fell on the floor exhausted, and she laughed and laughed and laughed.

Then someone laughed with her and said, "Try these. Great for hiccups and laughing jags." She swallowed two pink capsules, even though she had the impulse to say, "No thanks. I don't drink." She couldn't seem to form any words.

Later all she remembered was edging into a space on the floor and Donald holding her tight, and sometime later the dreams or the realities set in. She could never be sure which, because the dreams felt so real, and the realities were so completely dreamlike.

Sometimes when she seemed to wake, there were people all around her. All young. She saw no one as gurulike as William. They and she ate crackers and drank soft drinks out of bottles and talked and smoked. Whenever anyone handed around a joint, she took a drag or two. Sometimes the room and the lights and the faces spun around, and sometimes the faces were very still and enormous and silent in front of her. Always there was music, from far-out electronic sounds to the metallic precision of a harpsichord. What bothered her most was that every one of her senses seemed apart—nothing coordinated. Her ears were living one experience while her eyes led another and her body, her sense of touch, operated even more remotely.

Once when she became aware of her surroundings, the room was as dark as Oriana's cave, and she couldn't find a candle, and Donald's face was wet with either spilled Coke or sticky tears, and Wendy felt absurd because she couldn't tell which. The next time she woke, she knew Donald wasn't there. She crawled through all three rooms looking for him. He had left her, and her head ached violently again, and she was alone with complete strangers.

But she wasn't even that, she realized after a long while. She was completely alone on the couch in the living room. There wasn't another person in the place. There were just empty bottles, cigarette butts, and crumbs. And a clock that said ten o'clock.

Ten o'clock when? Wendy didn't care. She found some instant coffee and drank two mugs, strong and black. Then, soothed by the silence, she locked herself in the bathroom, washed her hair, and took a long, hot bath. As she was getting out of the tub, someone shook the doorknob. "I'll be right out," Wendy called. "Donald? Is that you?"

She hoped to hear his voice. Surely he had come back for her. But there was a strange silence, although she knew someone hesitated uneasily by the door. That frightened her, and she pulled her clothes on quickly, even though she hated the sticky touch of them. She wrapped her hair up in a towel turban and opened the door, still hoping to see Donald. But she saw a thin middle-aged woman, standing white-faced with her hand on the telephone, looking as frightened as Wendy and apparently ready to dial for help.

"What are you doing here?" Fear trembled in her voice. "How did you get in? Where is my nephew Charles? Are you a friend of Charles's?"

"I—just met him last night." Wendy couldn't remember whether she had ever actually met the Charlie people kept referring to as being somewhere in the crowded rooms—or not. But she sensed it would be better to say that she knew him. "There were quite a few people here, and it was rather late. I fell asleep—and didn't wake up until after Charlie had gone. I'm sorry if I scared you."

"It does look as if quite a few people were here, doesn't it? I've had to scold Charles three times lately about the mess he leaves the place in. I shan't let him have friends in any more when I go to the Cape weekends if he goes on this way. Especially if he's entertaining girls. You say there were three or four others here besides you?"

"Oh yes—all of that." Wendy was sure it must have been nearer thirty than three, but Charles's aunt apparently believed there was safety in numbers.

"Of course, I don't usually come back here until Monday night. I leave Friday morning for the office and take a bus after work and go right to the Cape. Then I come back early on the bus Monday and go right to work. But today I don't feel well, and I just can't go to work. Maybe Charles intended to come back and clean up before he thought I'd be home."

"Is this—Monday morning?"

"Of course."

"I'm a little mixed up. I thought it was Sunday." *Where did Sunday go?* The question bloomed in Wendy's mind, spelled out in enormous letters, surrounded by a black outline, like the dialogue of a comic-strip character. "Well, maybe that's where Charles is. Maybe that's where they all are. At work."

Except Donald. Where does Donald work?

"Charles doesn't work," explained his aunt. "He goes to Harvard. He will be a sophomore in the fall, but he failed a course, and he's making it up this summer. And taking something else, too. Although he doesn't talk about his classes very much."

"Why don't you let me clean up a little?" Wendy said, although she wondered if she could bend over without passing out. But the woman looked quite ill. "If you don't feel well, you must sit down and I'll go to it."

The woman, who also had a severe headache, lay on the couch, after asking Wendy to fix an ice-cold compress for her head. There wasn't an ice cube left, and the trays, half full of melted water, were on the kitchen floor for some reason. A great deal else was on the kitchen floor, too, and Wendy hoped the woman, who said she was Miss Kemmenth, would lie on the couch like an ostrich for at least two hours. It hurt Wendy's head to lean over, but she got used to it. She loathed cleaning at home and had worked out an elaborate system of bribes with her sisters, and even with the boys, to keep from doing just the kind of chores she was faced with now. But as she did it, she felt better. There was a kind of physical relief in taking the action. For the first time in days she even felt something like her old self. Yesterday she would have said that was bad. But today, she wondered a little. And what could have happened to Donald? How could he have left her? She was so sure from the words he had murmured to her that he cared for her just as much as she cared for him. And she wouldn't have left him!

By noontime she'd finished the kitchen and bathroom and the bedroom. There was just the living room. She persuaded Miss Kemmenth to move into bed and brought her tea and toast. Miss Kemmenth insisted Wendy make some for herself, too.

"Do you know, you are the first friend of Charles's I've met all summer? And I thoroughly approve, my dear. I hope he will bring you here often."

Wendy shifted uncomfortably, wondering which would make the woman feel worse—to have Wendy admit she was not really a friend of Charles's? Or to have Charles at some point looking very bewildered about some girl named Wendy? But Miss Kemmenth babbled on.

"I have been so apprehensive, because Cambridge has changed so that I don't even like to come into Harvard Square in the evening. Such odd-looking creatures about. But so far Charles has been at the library, studying he says, every evening and only comes in to use the couch in the living room quite late at night. Once he was so tired, poor boy, I found him on the floor with his head practically in the record player. But he's only brought his friends around while I'm away. I think he's rather ashamed of his Aunt Lillian. I guess I'm not quite—with it? Is that what they say now?"

Wendy smiled. She wondered what Charles could be like. He certainly believed in a different way of life from his Aunt Lillian.

By midafternoon Wendy had the place restored and refreshed, and knew Charles had been pretty lax in his previous pickings up, and that Aunt Lillian was either vainly nearsighted or quite uninterested in housekeeping herself. Wendy went into the bedroom to see if the woman wanted anything before she left.

"No, no. Thank you, my dear. But I shall certainly praise you to Charles. Wendy, isn't it? Such a pretty name. Do you live in Cambridge?"

"I'm staying in Boston. Let's see. Do I go to Harvard Square to take the subway?"

"Yes—that's the nearest."

Wendy felt in her pockets, just to check, and found to her horror all she had was a dime. She was sure she'd had three or four dollars in change with her. But of course she'd paid for four rides on the Swan Boat—that she remembered. And she'd bought the bread and bologna and cold drinks. And at the concert Donald had seen a friend and asked her for a dollar and come back with four joints—she remembered that. They smoked two at the concert and two on the bridge. Well, she'd have to borrow from Miss Kemmenth, but she still had some money in her rucksack even after paying Jez back for the earrings.

"Ooohhh!" Wendy clapped her hands to her ears. "My earrings. They've gone!" She had felt something was different when she washed her hair but been too groggy to realize what it was. Her wail of anguish was so real that Miss Kemmenth sat up.

"Did they fall off while you were cleaning?"

"They couldn't. My ears are pierced." She sat on the bed, fingering the tiny, empty holes in her ears, and suddenly a wave of nausea swept over her. She rushed into the bathroom and hung over the toilet, heaving. But it was dry heaves, emotional heaves. Her heart pounded and banged painfully in her chest, and she had trouble taking a breath. Yet she thought she wasn't really physically sick, despite the heaves and the faintness and the sweat that sprang out all over her.

It was her mind that was scaring her. Her mind was stuck. Her memory was blacking out, and she didn't want to set it going again.

Yet the next wave of blackness and nausea that swept through her must have been physical, for she suddenly threw up and hung, choking, over the toilet bowl.

She couldn't move for a long time, but she finally pulled herself together and looked up to see Miss Kemmenth hovering in the doorway, looking frightened.

Wendy hauled herself up. "I'm all right, really. I just kind of cleaned a little too fast maybe. Pushed myself too much when I was rather tired."

"I'm so sorry. You shouldn't have done it, after all. Where is that miserable Charles anyway! Come and sit down."

So the two of them sat in the dim living room, both feeling horrible, and stared at each other. Wendy knew she was still terrified and what terrified her was that she had been so unconscious of her self, her bodily self, that at some time during the long twenty-four hours of Sunday someone could have stolen the money out of her pockets and the earrings off her head—and she didn't even know it. They were the silver-and-garnet ones, and she knew she wouldn't have consciously parted with them for anyone.

Or would she have given them to Donald if he'd asked?

Perhaps she would have. She was that gone on him that in a hazy state she might have done anything he asked. And what things had he asked?

This new thought of what might have happened to her, that she just didn't remember, poured cold shivers down her spine and through her stomach again. Somewhere, with a clacking of train wheels to emphasize it, she heard Peter's voice telling her to watch it—that she might not always be in control of a situation. If Miss Kemmenth hadn't been staring helplessly at her, Wendy would have put her head down and bawled. She hadn't *felt* freaked out, she was sure. She didn't remember any particular physical actions or reactions. It was terribly frightening time lost and unaccounted for, and she had to find Donald to account for it. She had to know what had happened to her.

"Look. I've got to go. But I do need to borrow carfare from you. I guess I lost my money."

"Oh, my dear. Of course I'll give it to you. Hand me my purse."

The lady insisted on giving her a dollar. After all, she would have paid a cleaning lady six or seven times as much. "Where can I call you if I find your pocket-book or your earrings?" she asked.

Wendy realized for the first time she couldn't be reached by phone. Oriana didn't have one, and she didn't know the name of the person Zack sublet his apartment from. Instead of being glad she wasn't tied down to telephones and she could feel free of clutching familiar voices, she felt irritated and somewhat panicked. No one could reach her! How contradictory that was!

She thanked Miss Kemmenth for the money, took her street directions, and headed for Harvard Square. If she hadn't been upset about the earrings and her money and her lost self and Donald, she would have taken a detour through the Harvard yard. She'd been thinking about applying to Radcliffe, but she was frightened now to think ahead. Rolf and his timelessness and Donald and his nows-without-ifs was the only philosophy that applied. *Maybe that's what all that existentialism jazz we discussed in class was all about,* Wendy realized. *Maybe now I'm understanding it because I'm living it.*

The first thing she saw as she turned into Sage Lane was that Jez and Rolf sat on the front door step which amazed her. "Have you turned into the Fresh Air kids?"

Jez shrugged. "Oriana and William wanted the place to themselves for a while. Sit down."

"I just want to run up and check on something."

"Sit down and wait. Use your smarts."

"Oh."

Rolf moved over and she sat.

"Have you seen Donald?"

"No. But Nell was looking for him, too. All day Sunday. Making a very loud fuss. Maybe I should have warned you. She's Donald's protector."

"Does Donald need to be protected? By her? Or from her?"

"You'll have to answer that."

And that's what I can't answer, thought Wendy.

"Want a smoke?" Rolf asked.

"No, thanks."

"You are in a mood," said Jez. "Too bad! You missed a great party Saturday night. That's when it began, anyway. It really sort of went on till this morning, didn't it, Rolf?"

"Yes. It must be a Monday today. Mondays are awkward days. Artificial days. Everybody gets hung up on Mondays because they're supposed to be a beginning. And who wants to begin anything?"

But Wendy couldn't be diverted into one of Rolf's useless discussions. "Has Peter come back?"

"As a matter of fact he did come in last night," Jez remembered. "And he was livid because no one knew where you were. That made Oriana furious. Remember Rolf? She was stoned, really stoned, has been for two days. But not stoned enough not to tell Peter off."

"Oh?" Wendy laughed. She remembered how much she'd felt Peter needed to be shot down—and she was sorry she hadn't been around to see it.

"Oriana stood on the couch and draped the cover around her and posed like the Statue of Liberty and said 'Listen everybody. I am Freedom. I am Liberty. But I am not a Den Mother.' She was superb, wasn't she, Rolf?"

Rolf laughed. "She could be in the theater. Any time."

"Then what did Peter do?"

"He left."

Wendy sat uncomfortably on the steps. She didn't feel like idling away time until Oriana and William opened the door. She wanted to start searching for Donald. But she wanted to get her money first. She vaguely felt she could tell Nell to leave Donald alone if she knew she had the money to take care of him. And until she'd talked to Donald, she didn't want to see Peter at all.

But before too long William and Oriana came out. Oriana wore a short black linen dress with a white yoke, which not only looked expensive but as if it had just come from the cleaners. Her hair was beautifully done in a twist. She carried an expensive black lizard bag and wore little-heeled shoes to match.

"I'm going to see William off on the bus and then go collect the rent money. I'll be back, Jez. Wendy, Peter was looking for you."

"I heard. I don't know why he should fuss about me, though."

"You'll have to straighten that out with him. I don't like fusses. They upset William. So he's going back to the farm."

"I'm sorry!" Wendy apologized. "It's been wonderful to know you, William."

"You think about some of those precepts we discussed," William told her, earnestly scowling at her. "You'll find after a while you must agree with me, I'm sure."

Wendy nodded, feeling dumb but not much caring. Oriana put a hand on his arm and drew him off down the Lane. They made quite a contrast—William unkempt and shambling and Oriana looking like a model.

"Why does she dress up like that to collect the rent?" Wendy asked. "And where, if she's so broke, did she ever get those clothes?"

"Those are in a box marked 'Do Not Sell.' She keeps it under the couch. Her father's lawyer makes her come to his office once a month. If she looks either ratty or happy, he lectures her for an hour. But if she dresses up and looks as if she were grimly and puritanically busy at some social-service type job, he smiles and hands her the check. She signs it, hands it back, and then he gives her some cash, and he pays the rental agent the rest. She used to balk and carry on and tell him what a hypocrite he was and how he represented all the worst of his generation and the Establishment. But she found he looked forward to lecturing her and left the door open to his office, so his secretaries could hear the lecture, too. So Oriana said she'd fix that. She just goes in looking that way and takes the wind out of his sails."

"Good for her!" Wendy ran up to the apartment and for the second time in one day stepped into the aftermath of a weekend pot-and-pill party. There were Coke bottles, unwashed dishes, cushions, ash trays, butts, a paperback book which had been torn out of its binding and handed around in shredding sections, pieces of clothing, and apple cores—all in one grand mishmash over the couches and rug. Jez and Rolf followed Wendy and both settled down into a nest of oddments, ignoring the mess. Wendy was disgusted.

When she saw her lute out of its case, lying in a corner with a string broken, she yelled even louder than she did when she discovered her earrings gone. "Who took out my lute! Who dared! Jez! Rolf! You know I never, never let anyone touch it."

"William wanted to use it. One of his friends who stopped by was a musicologist. Oriana didn't think you'd mind if a famous musicologist used it."

"A musicologist isn't a musician. He broke a string."

"Oh, he didn't break it. It broke later on. Someone else was playing it then."

"I see. A good, free time for all with anybody's things!" Wendy stamped her foot.

"You know what!" Rolf said. "You've got the worst hang-up on *things*."

"We argued about that when I first came," Wendy reminded him. "My lute is more than—an old *thing*."

"It is essentially a materialistic possession," Rolf argued. He grinned wickedly. He enjoyed stirring Wendy up.

"It is capable of being far more—so it isn't just that," Wendy insisted. "It can be music. But I guess you wouldn't understand that fine point. And where did my rucksack go? I left it under that couch. It's not there."

"It might be in the bathroom," Jez suggested. "I think I saw a girl take it in there. Said she was looking for soap."

"I'll bet." Wendy found it behind the toilet. It was very lightweight as she picked it up.

She brought it into the big room and deliberately sat down. She pulled things out and piled them on the couch. Bikini underwear, bikini, sweater, dress. All the clothing was there. But her money, her red-silk sari scarf, and her silver-studded Navaho belt were gone. The box of earrings had been opened. She knew be-

cause the heavy elastic she used to keep it closed since
the clasp broke was missing. Carefully she looked
through it, pairing up the earrings and counting them.
She'd had twenty-two pairs. Now there were twenty.
A pair of gold studs and a pair of large gold-finished
Portuguese earrings were missing.

"I've been robbed," she said, and burst into tears.

12

"WHAT ARE you crying about!" Rolf was disgusted. "Don't we all manage to get along without money and things?"

"That's easy for you to say," Wendy accused him. "If this is supposed to be everybody helping everybody else, you're the only one I've never seen contribute anything. Not once. But you eat up and smoke up what other people provide. And take advantage of Oriana's roof."

"Rolf worked for two months this spring!" Jez defended him. "He contributed every cent of his pay to Oriana. He could have gone on unemployment, too, you know. But he didn't."

"Oh? Why not?"

"It's immoral," said Rolf. "For anyone my age."

"I'm glad you have some principles."

"I have a lot of principles. I'm not selling my soul to any Establishment. I just intend to be me and nothing else. Now, what higher principle is there than that?"

"The principles may be all right," Wendy sniffed. "But the methods aren't. Most of the time you're doing absolutely nothing. How can you get anywhere that way?"

"Get *where?*" Rolf was indignant, and for once there seemed to be a healthier flush in his yellowish-white face.

"Oh, I give up. But in the meantime, I need my money. And it's gone. And so are my most expensive earrings."

"I don't know who used your cash, Wendy, but here's your earrings. I borrowed them." Jez pulled them out of her jeans' pocket. "I wore them this weekend. A friend of mine was here from Jersey, and I felt, you know—like I wanted to look glamorous."

Poor stumpy Jez, Wendy thought. *She's such a lump I've misjudged her.* "That's all right, Jez. Hope it worked."

"It must have. He wanted me to go back to Jersey with him."

"Why didn't you?"

"I'm happier here. Oriana's easier to get along with than he would be. And once in a while she needs me."

"She seems so self-sufficient."

"I know. But just every now and then, she really needs me. If she has a bad trip I'm the only one who can help. I started to be a nurse. I had two years of training actually." Jez spoke with a trace of pride in her voice that Wendy hadn't heard before, and she was surprised. Jez had seemed like such a nonperson, just kind of an automatic do-what-Oriana-said machine, who never talked about herself.

Wendy put the dangling earrings away and slipped the gold studs into her ears. But that didn't solve her problem of money and what she was going to live on— let alone how she could help Donald or wean him away from Nell. She sat there, frowning, realizing that she hadn't minded contributing to the communal pot in this informal household as long as she held something back for herself. She had not been ready to throw everything in. And she couldn't trustfully throw herself into the group and expect to be taken care of by hook or by crook—something inside just wouldn't let her. The old cliché phrase that had popped into her mind, "by hook or by crook," seemed suddenly horribly appropriate. She felt very uneasy.

Sadly she rescued her lute, noting which string was broken. Maybe she could borrow some money from Peter for that. He would know how much it meant to her. And she could pay Peter back when she went home.

It was the first time she'd said "when she went home" out-loud in her mind. Of course she'd expected to return in time to get herself ready for her last year at Parsley. She never once intended not to go back and finish there. But she wasn't so sure now she wanted to rush on through the competing insanity to college. She'd felt that way even before taking off to test her independence. But when she'd mentioned working for Vista for a year to her parents, their reaction hadn't been encouraging.

Yet when she left Meridian Farm, it had been with the idea that she was completely capable of taking care of herself for the summer, and she would return triumphant after at least six weeks on her own. She had seen herself walking in, tanned and serene, intact and cool, to impress her parents with her new maturity. And with a few other adventures, perhaps, for her sisters' ears only. It had all been so easy to imagine. But her imagination had fallen short on the details of real, everyday existence. It would be very humiliating to return to Meridian Farm penniless and in a panic, after only a week. She just couldn't do it. Somehow, she'd have to stick it out. But how? Sell her gold earrings to Mr. Volmarr, if his shop were still open? See if the Public Garden ever hired girl Swan-Boat pedalers? She felt very frustrated.

She closed the lute case and slid it under the couch. "I'm going down to see if Peter's around."

Wendy knocked on Zack's door, but no one came to open it. *Oh, zap!* said Wendy. *Just when I really need Peter after all.*

She impatiently shook the doorknob, and the door unexpectedly opened.

"Anyone in?" she called. "Peter? Zack?"

Maybe Zack was in his closet-size darkroom doing some timed work and couldn't come out or didn't hear her. She knocked but no one was in there. As she passed the big desktable where Zack often worked, she saw a print of a girl laughing. It was one of the shots he'd taken of her. For once she was pleased, because even though her mouth was open, she didn't look too idiotic. Then she realized that all the pictures spread out on the table were of her and they were pasted on pieces of paper with captions typed below.

Her name did not appear, but the captions obviously carried on the picture story of a young girl leaving home to become a hippie. She had never dreamed Zack was so omnipresent or so clever in taking her picture unaware. She hadn't realized he'd been nearby when she lay on the grass, listening to Donald read French poetry. There was Nell in the picture, too, distinctive in her hat and scarf, with the pigeons winging about in the background. And there Wendy was playing her lute, with Jez's stoned face blown up and floating in the background. That was a montage, she was sure. There was a print of the group of them on the stairs, listening to Rolf. And strangely enough—there she was drowsing on a bench. But that wasn't the Common or the Public Garden. That was Washington Square in New York.

Peter must have taken that. She remembered the heavy pendant he'd worn on a chain around his neck. It must have had a camera in it. But he hadn't worn it once since he'd teamed up with Zack. They were working together on some kind of magazine or newspaper article, and she was the subject. The innocent bird!

She was furious. Peter should have been honest and asked her permission. Zack had, although he hadn't honestly told her what the pictures were for.

She poked around some more and came up with a manuscript of about thirty typewritten pages. At first glance she thought it was Peter's essay to go with the pictures. Then she realized it was a typed transcription of her conversation with Peter on the train. And of the conversation she'd had with him here in this very apartment after she'd met Jez and Rolf. She could still hear herself saying those things, and the biggest jolt was that they didn't always read as she had meant them. The words on the page had no tone of voice to rescue a meaning. It made her sound so naïve and goody-goody she felt sick.

But how had Peter done the taping—especially on the train? She sat down to think and her foot kicked something under the table. It was Peter's ever-present zipper bag. She pulled it out and there, small and neat, was a tape recorder. She remembered his business of digging around in the bag for cigarettes and even going off for a smoke. What he'd been doing was turn on the recorder and then change the tape. She was a dope and a dupe. She didn't want her naïveté splashed on public pages anywhere. Her family would hate it, and she could never go back to Parsley. Just who did Peter Banbury think he was! She could sue him.

Or she could mess it up for him—that was her original idea. To find out what he was up to and foil him. She grabbed the transcript, tore it into pieces, and flung the pieces all over the room. *They'll never put that back together again.*

Except for the stupid tapes. Where were they? She opened drawers in the desk, looked on shelves and behind books, searched the kitchen and bathroom. She hesitated again by the table, realizing the most identifying aspect of all was her pictures. But it is almost impossible for a woman, especially one who is young and photogenic, to destroy her own pictures. Candid as they were, Zack had caught Wendy's feelings over and over again—and their expression fascinated her.

She was still by the table when a key was inserted in the lock and the door pushed open. It was Peter. He saw her and stood there, completely dismayed.

"I wish I could take a picture of your face right now!" Wendy yelled at him. "What do you think you're doing to me!"

"How did you get in here? You aren't supposed to see—any—of that—yet."

"The door was unlocked. Someone left in a hurry and it didn't latch. But how could you, Peter! How could you use me that way! Just to make money and sell it to a magazine? What magazine? *True Confessions!*"

"Listen, Wendy—sit down and listen. It isn't for a magazine. I promise you. And I was going to show it to you before I handed it in. But I couldn't tell you about it beforehand because your reactions wouldn't have been natural—"

"*Hand it in!* If it isn't a magazine, it's a newspaper then! That's ten times worse." She grabbed some of the pasted-up pages and threw them in his face as she ran out the door.

She slammed the door of Oriana's apartment and locked it. "Don't let Peter in," she ordered Jez. For once Rolf wasn't seated on the hassock, so she drew it to the window and sat there, looking out, letting the tears, blackened with eyeliner, run clownishly down her face.

Peter pounded on the door and pushed at it. "Wendy! You've got to let me talk to you."

Wendy sat gulping and sniffing, and when Jez started to open the door, she begged, "*Please* don't. I hate him and I don't trust him, and I don't want to see him at all."

Rolf said, "I don't trust that guy either. He's been up

to visit Zack off and on for a month, but he's been much too curious about everyone. He spent one whole evening up here before Oriana went away last time asking all kinds of questions."

"He probably had a tape recorder in his pocket."

"Could be. He wasn't writing anything down. But he certainly was full of questions."

"Do you think he's fuzz or a Fed?" asked Jez.

"I'm sure he's not police," said Wendy. "I heard him quitting a job on Wall Street, and he couldn't have been working there and been a policeman at the same time."

"He could be a Fed. Attached to a rackets squad or something. Maybe he was investigating a stock fraud and then got reassigned to some other racket. But what would that have to do with us?"

"Oh, wow!" Jez looked stunned. "I hope he's never looked in that suitcase. Did you ever tell him about selling those things for me, Wendy?"

"No. Why?"

"Because I don't exactly have a great-aunt whose things I inherited. They're more like—a present from a friend in Jersey. Every time he comes up, he brings me some things he doesn't want to sell around there. And I don't know where he gets them because he purposely doesn't tell me. I'm just supposed to share some of the money with him, if I do sell them."

"You mean that the stuff I took into Mr. Volmarr's shop was probably stolen? Is that what you aren't quite saying?" Wendy demanded.

"Possibly," Jez admitted.

"How absolutely glorious!" Wendy sat there, feeling sick. She imagined her parents' reaction, first, to their daughter's notorious appearance in print, and then to the news she'd been arrested for selling stolen property. What if Peter was a Fed? And his story and pictures was just a cover? Wendy wished now she hadn't panicked and had stayed long enough to hear what he had to say.

There was another impatient knock on the door, but it was Oriana. Jez let her in. Wendy said, "Oh—never mind locking the door again. I should go and talk to Peter."

"What's going on?" asked Oriana, putting down a bag of groceries.

"Peter Banbury has been working on some kind of article about me, taping a lot of stuff I've said, and having Zack take pictures. I saw it downstairs. He never asked me if he could. But we don't know if he's fuzz or a Fed. Or if the article and interviews are a cover for some investigation. Or if he's a real reporter or a writer."

Oriana laughed. "Peter would do almost anything to escape being a stockbroker and a partner in his father's company. That's his father's fondest wish—to be Banbury and Son, Brokers. But I don't think Peter would go as far as being a cop or a detective. He isn't hard enough. After all, I've fought with him since we were little kids. I know."

"I thought he just met you in the Village last summer," Wendy said.

"Is that what he told you? It's not true. His family and my family had beachhouses side by side on Martha's Vineyard for years. I've stomped on his sand castles, and he's pushed me into big cold waves since we were four years old. I quit being brainwashed by summer vacations with parents when I was fifteen and refused to sit around being social. So I didn't see him for a few years, until he bumped into me last summer in the Village. It was sticky, because he decided the reason he'd teased me all those years was because he was in love with me. But he was just reacting against all of his parents' wishes. And he knew that they knew my family had disowned me. As much as I disown them. All that social crap is a waste of life. So he thought if he brought me home as his hippie-love, they'd throw him out, too. And no more beating on him to be 'and Son.' But Peter isn't the one for me. He's just kind of a square idealist who hangs around the fringes doing wishful thinking and not wanting either to conform—or to be an activist. He's just kind of wishy-washy."

"I wish we'd recorded what you just said on tape. To play back to him," said Wendy bitterly. "I'd like to see him react to your calling him wishy-washy."

Oriana laughed. "I called him that last summer. He reacted all right. He took some acid and had a bad trip. It scared him so he swears he hasn't touched the stuff since. He's afraid to live. Wendy, you look like an op-art portrait with those black tear stains striping your face."

"Ugh." Wendy shut herself in the bathroom, and forgetting she'd already had a bath in Cambridge, took a shower. While it was running, she cried good and hard. *I'll go down and tell Peter he is a wishy-washy skunk, as well as a reject of Oriana's,* she decided. *And if he doesn't give me the tapes and the negatives and tear up the prints I'll—I'll what?* What could she do? What strengths could she draw on—when she'd just been on a lost weekend and discovered she'd been disposing of stolen property?

She'd just have to go and beg him to give the tapes and pictures to her. But then he'd think she was ashamed of walking out on her family and trying to be a hippie. And she wasn't. She really wasn't. Maybe worried. But not ashamed.

But it was her private business and her private life. Peter and his tape recorder and Zack and his camera had no right to make any of it public.

Absent-mindedly she got her hair wet again in the shower. She rubbed it enough so it didn't drip and put on her dress. Somehow blue jeans didn't suit the mood she was in. She changed to the dangling gold earrings. She carefully made up her eyes.

When she walked through the living room Rolf whistled and tried to pull her down beside him on the couch. For all his unhealthy look, he had strong hands, and her wrist felt bruised after she wrenched away from his grip. "I'm off on business. Don't stop me."

"If it's to tell off Peter, you can tell him off for me, too," Rolf said. "He really is a snot."

On her way down the stairs again, Wendy remembered her original errand had been to borrow money from Peter—for a lute string. Perhaps she still would. But she could hardly ask him for money to live on. *How mixed up things are,* she thought. *A little thing like a lute string gets to be vital. But the big things are so confusing I don't even want to try to cope with them now.*

She knocked, expecting Peter to fly to the door. To her surprise a complete stranger opened the door. He was a balding young man, rather chunky, and although she didn't know who he was, he seemed to be expecting her.

"Are you Wendy from upstairs? Peter thought you might stop by."

"Is he here?"

"No. But come in anyway."

She hesitated, and he realized she was upset. "It's all right. I don't bite. My name is Allan Westbox, and actually this is my apartment. My work brought me back a month early from the West Coast, and Zack is very kind. He's going to let me share my own apartment with him until his sublet runs out."

As Wendy stepped in, she saw the table had been cleared of Peter's work. The papers and pictures were gone. Except for a few elusive scraps of the ripped papers she'd flung about, there was no trace of her tantrum. Peter's zipper bag was also gone.

"How about a cold Coke?" Allan suggested.

"No thanks. Is Peter coming back shortly? I have to see him."

"No. But he left me a message to give you." Allan took a piece of paper off the shelf by the phone and handed it over.

Wendy sat on the couch and read: "Dear Wendy, I promise you that the material you saw is not for publication, although I have to admit there is a purpose behind it. I want to see you and talk to you about it. Will be back in a couple of days. Meantime, stay put, will you? Even if Oriana is a kook. Zack will be around, but don't take your fight out on him. He's a pacifist, remember? Fight with me. I will return. Love, Peter."

13

Love, Peter! Wendy noted. *Who does he think he is anyway?* All the feelings she had about his arrogance when they met came rushing back. But she hadn't succeeded in shooting him down. He was still flying around all over the place. She was the one who'd been wounded—shot down as successfully as the real Wendy pinged with an arrow by the Lost Boys.

The real Wendy! What am I thinking of! Wendy felt a tremor of fear shoot through her stomach. *How can I mix up that stupid Peter Pan business and think of that Wendy as real! I must be out of my trees!*

Wendy's head hurt and she felt woozy, too. She couldn't seem to think straight at all.

Allan handed her a glass of cold Coke. "Sip. You may not want it, but you look as if you need something. Are you hungry?"

"Oh, I don't know. I did have some lunch—some tea and toast." *But I tossed it up later, and there were about thirty-six hours in there, between picnicking on the Charles River bank Saturday and the tea and toast on Monday, that I don't remember eating anything but pills—and munching things. But munching what? Chips? Crackers? Hashish cookies? More pills?*

"Look—" Allan sat beside her. "What can I do to help? You really seem upset."

"No," Wendy insisted. "I'm not upset. I can cope. But I'm mad at Peter. And I guess I can't straighten that out till I see him. But I'm really all right."

I am all right she insisted to herself. *I am. I will be. I can take care of myself, and Donald.*

"Maybe you could do something for me, though. I seem to have lost my wallet. I came down to see if Peter would lend me some money. I want to buy a lute string."

"That's an unusual request." Allan stood up and reached into his back pocket for his wallet. He handed her a ten-dollar bill.

"Lute strings don't cost that much."

"No. But Peter left that for you. He said it was an 'emergency fund' for Wendy."

"I won't take it. Forget it. A lute string isn't an emergency. And I don't want to be part of any emergency fund." Wendy was embarrassed, and she could feel her eyes getting teary. It was horrible—her tendency to weep over any little thing. She never used to be that way. Even worse, she couldn't sort out her feelings. She was cross one minute and giggly the next. She didn't know if she wanted to cry because she was mad or sorry for herself—or both.

"How much is a lute string?" Allan asked, ignoring her shiny eyes.

"Not more than two dollars."

"I'll loan it to you." He put the ten back and handed her some change instead. "Don't forget about this, though. Peter told me to keep an eye out for you."

"Oh, goody for him. What time is it?"

"About five."

"That music store on Boylston Street may still be open if I rush."

"Right." Allan closed the door behind her, and Wendy, as she started down the stairs, heard him dial

a phone number. She wondered how far Peter's trip
really was taking him.

Happily she reached the store in time, and they had
the right string. She slowly sauntered back through the
Common, searching every knot of people for Donald,
or even Nell. She walked along Charles Street, noting
everyone on the sidewalks. This was the hour when
Nell was often out panhandling. But if she'd ended up
with Wendy's earrings and sold them somewhere, perhaps she wouldn't need to be out begging today.
Wendy glanced down at Mr. Volmarr's shop, even
hoping to see the earrings back in the window. But
they weren't. Wendy knew she couldn't go in there
again because she couldn't look Mr. Volmarr in the
eye any more.

When she reached the apartment, Oriana had
packed her good clothes away in her Do-Not-Sell box
and was back in her crumpled purple tunic again.

"Why are you so fond of purple?" Wendy asked.

"I don't know. It just makes me feel comfortable. Do
you have to have a reason for everything? That's so
suburban."

"What do you mean suburban?"

"So amateur psychology. You know, all the parents
and teachers take courses and read books and pick up
phrases. So you grow up not being able to do anything
without being analyzed and discussed and told why
you do it. Who cares? I just do something because I
like to. Or because my aunt belonged to a class at college that had to wear purple gym tunics, and I found
it in a box, and it's comfortable. You know—let them
make something out of that if they want. They're
stupid."

"What else was in the box?" Wendy asked, thinking
of the costume trunk in the attic of Meridian Farm and
how Oriana would revel in it.

"Horrible artifacts like dried-up corsages and scrib-
bled-in yearbooks and letters from boys and diaries.

My aunt would die if she knew I'd been rooting around in her youth. That's why you shouldn't ever leave untidy pieces of yourself around. I don't. I could put everything I possess in three cartons and be gone tomorrow. It's great. Nothing clutching me. No hang-ups. Rolf's even better organized. He doesn't even need a carton.

"Why?"

"You see me with all I possess." Rolf stood up and bowed. "I am wearing my total wardrobe. I have a tobacco pouch and a package of cigarette papers and a social-security card. They fit in my pockets. What else do I need?"

"Not even a draft card?" Wendy wondered.

"I've been. I'm through. I spent two years in the Army. One in Vietnam. Where do you think I found out I don't believe in anything except that they really will drop The Bomb someday and Zap! End of world. Where do you think I picked up malaria? Oh, yes. One more possession. I do keep a pocketful of antimalaria pills. They mix pretty well with the other kinds. Where do you think I began smoking pot? Out in the bush on the Cambodian border. That's where I began smoking pot. Any ambition I ever had got drained right out of me in one year. All I care about is no one bugging me from day to day. Man, that's all that feels good."

"How old are you anyway?" Wendy asked. The old-youngness of Rolf had baffled her all along.

"Twenty-one, actually. One hundred and two mentally. And about seventy physically. I spent six months in the hospital when I came back."

"With malaria?"

"Among other things. I had competing fevers. I'm just a burned-out case, so what does it matter if I keep going up in smoke or what the smoke's from?"

"You don't say much about Vietnam. I didn't even realize you'd been out there."

"You don't just *say* about it, like show-and-tell. The

only ones who've got strength enough to tell about it
are those who haven't been there. I just don't want to
remember it or talk about it. I want to turn it all off.
Hey, Oriana—how's funds? I need to look up my guy
down on Charles. This is his night to be around."

"Look in the sugar jar. Help yourself. Jez, you might
go along, too. See what you can do for all of us."

While Rolf and Jez went off to forage, Wendy re-
strung her lute and settled down to playing and singing. Oriana hummed happily as she peeled potatoes
and patted out some spicy hamburgers. *She is an odd
combination,* Wendy thought. *Always scrubbing her
face and washing her hands like Lady Macbeth.* Yet
content with a cocoon of clothing—her purple tunic—
that she didn't have to fuss with. Willing to put her
own principles on the legal line, as if she could lead
a crusade; yet wily enough to deceive her father's lawyer without any scruples at all. *How does she sort herself out with herself?* Wendy wondered. *Or is she like
Rolf really, and all she cares about is day-to-day survival and no one bugging her? Is that what their lives
are going to be every day for years and years and years?
Where is the better, more-aware, more-alive person
they keep telling me an expanded consciousness is supposed to make?*

When Rolf and Jez came back, Oriana cooked the
hamburgers, which were delicious. Wendy cleaned up
afterward.

"Anyone want to go to the Common to see what's
happening?" she asked.

"Someone told me there's a strict curfew now," said
Oriana. "Everybody off the Common by midnight. And
the police are out to enforce it."

"Whatever for?"

"They're so afraid of trouble that they're making
trouble," Jez said. "It happens all the time, doesn't it!
If they'd just leave us alone, we wouldn't bother anybody."

"Robbie told me the Board of Health has been poking around the place he and Charlene have been using lately—over in Cambridge. Something about too many people and insanitary conditions and disease. And nobody's causing any trouble at all. They're just *living* there."

"A lot of people in a small place?" Wendy asked.

"I suppose you could call twenty or so people a lot in a three-room apartment. He and Charlene may come back here tonight, Oriana."

Oriana shrugged. "They know how to get in. I'm not going to the Common. I'm going to meditate for a while." She put on a Ravi Shankar record, took out a white clay pipe and tucked some grass neatly into its small bowl, and sat on the floor in the lotus position, looking up at her psychedelic poster.

Wendy opened her mouth to ask Oriana something, but Jez raised her finger to her lips and shook her head. So Wendy didn't ask. But she really wanted to know why Oriana did everything at once—the music, the pot, the poster, the lotus position—to meditate? Weren't they contradictory and confusing? *It's like lighting a candle, praying, carrying a rabbit's foot and a security blanket, and reading your horoscope for the day all at the same time,* she realized. *If Oriana has to go through all that ritual to turn on, isn't she hung-up on it?*

"I'll take a walk with you," Rolf said, and Jez decided to go, too.

It was a good summer night, warm with a slight breeze, and all ages of people were out to enjoy it. Younger ones stood about on the Common in clusters, holding what seemed to be earnest discussion groups. Others sat in impromptu song fests. They paid no attention to the ring of lookers-on. There were hecklers and toughs, but unless they found some of their own kind to egg on, they met little response. Wendy noticed, however, that there were more policemen than usual.

Rolf tried to keep Wendy with him when he stopped to join some friends. But she wanted to look for Donald. "I'll be back," she told him.

"Huh. That's what you said before you disappeared for two days."

"Oh, don't worry."

"Worry about you? Miss Coldly Competent of 1968? Hardly." He turned his back on her after all. Wendy knew then that she had a problem with Rolf, and staying on at Oriana's wasn't going to keep on being an easy situation.

Jez walked along with her.

"Did you ever think of flinging yourself madly at Rolf?" Wendy asked Jez hopefully.

"I did. But that's all over. We had ourselves real hung-up on each other for three months. I liked him while he was working. But when he stopped and was around all the time, we got tired of each other, I guess. So he goes his way and I go mine, even if we still stay in the same place."

"And it doesn't bother you? You're not in love with him any more?"

"Maybe I wasn't really in love with Rolf ever. He was handy. We kept each other warm at night, so to speak. I still like my friend in Jersey better. Do you like Rolf? Does my being around bother you?"

"Oh, no! I'm glad you're there. I don't want Rolf to get hung-up on me at all. I don't feel very comfortable alone with him now. He bugs me. Actually, Jez, I'm looking for Donald Milner, Nell's friend. I've got to find him. Will you help me look?"

"So that's the way it is. I'll help you, but I wish you luck."

"Why? Because of Nell?"

"Oh, Nell. You *know* what she's like. But Donald never seems for real somehow."

"What do you mean?"

"I saw some kids too much like him when I was in

training in a psychiatric ward. Real schizos. That was what turned me off nursing—being in that ward. I just couldn't stand kids tearing themselves apart like that."

"But Donald's not crazy, Jez!" Wendy protested. "He's moody, maybe. But so are lots of people. But he couldn't be crazy—he's so warm and loving. He's so easy to relate to."

"Well—you see what you want to see," said Jez stubbornly. Suddenly she gave a start. "That looks like Nell over there."

They plunged off into the crowd. Wendy followed and was caught up in a group happily playing Blind Man's Buff. A girl who looked like a gypsy in a multicolored flounced skirt, a whirling sash, and a blouse with drooping sleeves, had a black scarf tied over her eyes. Hands reaching out, her waist-length black hair flying about as she lunged out to catch someone, she was laughing. She made a handsome picture as her friends dodged about, whistling or calling to tease her. Wendy paused. She couldn't help grinning, because this didn't seem to be a put on. Here were kids her own age and a little older, unselfconsciously playing a children's game and having a ball. But she paused too long, and suddenly the girl reached out and tagged her.

"Oh!" Wendy said in surprise and pulled away. "I wasn't playing."

"No one was when we started," the girl giggled. "But it's more fun than group therapy." The girl whipped the scarf off, and a boy leaped over to help tie it over Wendy's eyes before she could twist away. The agony of it was that Wendy was sure she'd just seen Donald at the edge of the crowd. She fought to free herself, and the boy, tying the knot so tight that he pulled her hair, said, "What's the matter? Don't you know how to turn on and have fun?"

The scarf had an acrid dirty smell, and Wendy shoved at it so she could breathe.

"No cheating!" someone yelled and poked at her.

Wendy whirled furiously. Why had she thought they were having a ball? Why had the game looked like fun, till someone made her do it? Her fingers hit a trousered leg that promptly slid away.

"Run! Run! You can't catch me!" someone teased. How weird the voices sounded—as if they were distorted on tape that was speeded up.

"Here I am!" A boy's voice bounced close and faded off. It was so like Donald, Wendy gasped and reached out, pleading.

This is ridiculous! All I have to do is snatch off this blindfold and say I won't play. I don't want to play with you! Wendy thought. But she couldn't do it. She'd been conditioned not to be a poor sport. *Even though it makes me a fool!*

The only thing to do was get it over with quickly. Catch someone and be done. She leaped about in a frenzy. It was impossible in such a small space that she couldn't find a victim—unless they had all on a signal run away, like a scene in some surrealist movie.

Then a boy making a quick dodge in front of her stubbed his bare toe and dropped to the grass. She fell on top of him. "You're it! You're it!" she shrieked and wrenched off the scarf, pulling her hair painfully. The minute she had it off and saw all the laughing kids around her, she was embarrassed at how furious she'd felt. The boy she'd caught sat grinning and groaning over his bent toe. She thrust the scarf at him, and he meekly took it to tie over his eyes.

Wendy quickly pushed her way out of the circle, but Donald, if it had been he, was gone. She heard some shouting and saw a rush of people near the corner of the Common, but she went on sifting through the crowd. She wanted to call out, "Donald! Where are you, Donald!" But she didn't dare.

The shouting grew louder, and a siren screamed as a patrol wagon pulled in at the curb. Wendy found her-

self suddenly pushed along in a crush of kids running
to see what was happening.

"Fuzz!" someone yelled. "They're going to throw us
off the Common. Don't let 'em."

A police officer bellowed at the crowd through a bull
horn. "You will clear the Common, please. The curfew
is midnight and the Common must be cleared. Move
along. Move along quietly and no one will get hurt."

But just then someone, probably a heckler out to stir
things up, threw a full beer can at a policeman. It
struck him on the back of the head, and he went down
with a sickening thud. Immediately the police seemed
to grow in numbers and to reach out with as many arms
apiece as an Eastern idol. Spectators shrieked and tried
to dash out of the way. Hippies who felt dislodged and
harassed and wanted to protest ill treatment lurched
around shouting. Police moved in without listening and
popped them into the patrol wagon. Hecklers were
caught, too. Wendy was pushed nearer and nearer the
action, which was violent. People and police chased
each other, yelled, screeched, and threw things. She
tried to turn and get out of the mess to where she could
stand alone and catch her breath, but she was trapped.

Suddenly someone grabbed her arm and pulled her
sideways, bulldozing an opening out of the crowd. It
was Rolf. He succeeded in freeing her, and finally they
reached open space in the street. Traffic was halted.
Some drivers quickly locked their car doors and rolled
up the windows as a protection against flying missiles.
Others rolled their windows down and hung out, yelling at whichever side they hated—cops or hippies.
Wendy, gasping, was frightened. All the whacking, the
thud of a stick or a fist on flesh, made her feel sick.

"Oh, Rolf! Why do people have to be so hateful to
each other. All the kids were doing was having fun. Or
just hanging around. Why do they have to fight about
it?"

Rolf held her tightly, still protecting her although no

one was near them. She saw his eyes squinted, steely, and he hurt her he was holding her so rigidly. "If this makes you sick, you should see people kill each other."

"Oh, no!" Wendy yelled. "There's Nell and Donald. Donald!" She tried to pull free from Rolf, but he wouldn't let her go. He didn't even seem to hear her. He'd slipped into some kind of memory that thundered in his mind with horror and reflected in terror on his face. His hands on her arm were like a steel ring.

Wendy screamed and pulled as she saw one policeman carrying Nell by the arms and another by the feet. Nell was shouting at them, but helpless. They threw her into the patrol wagon and slammed the door. Then she saw that Donald had slipped free. He was running. He crossed the street, and Wendy thought he was coming to her. "Donald! Over here. It's Wendy."

But Donald, unseeing, ran past her, ten feet away, and dashed down one of the paths into the Public Garden.

"Rolf, please let me go," Wendy begged. But he still didn't see her or hear her. As one of the wagons started up with a screech of its siren and flashing of the eerie-blue eye on its roof, Rolf suddenly picked Wendy up, flung her over his shoulder and plunged into the traffic to cross the corner of Beacon and Charles. Cars had started to move, and Wendy was terrified to find herself with her breath almost crushed out by Rolf's sudden action, head bobbing down over his back, eyes blinking in the stabbing glare of car headlights that seemed to rush at her like wild animals in a jungle. He dodged and ran as cars honked at him, a policeman whistled at him, and braked tires shrieked.

The next thing Wendy knew she was braced against a brick wall on Beacon Street, with Rolf's big body covering her, his arms cradling her head so she could hardly breathe. He was muttering over and over, "It's all right. You're safe. They'll stop the shelling soon. I'll keep you safe."

Then Wendy realized the noise and the lights and the rushing people must have triggered some memory from Vietnam, and he'd been caught up in a nightmare of reaction. She pulled herself together. "Look Rolf. It's Wendy. You're right here in Boston. There's nothing wrong. It's not the war at all."

"Oh, yes it is. It's all back again. I want to go home."

"Come on, Rolf. I'll get you home."

She led him along, wondering where his home really was. *Maybe the Midwest somewhere from the way he rolled his "r's." What did he think of when he said home, though? Oriana's cavernous flat? Or some white-frame farmhouse on a prairie?*

By the time she pushed him up the stairs, he was shivering. Oriana sat on the floor, no longer in the lotus position, but arms around her legs, head down on her knees, unaware of their noisy entrance. The record player for some reason hadn't shut itself off, and the needle was scratching around in its final, soundless grooves, over and over.

"Of all the times to be far out in a trance!" Wendy said, hoping Oriana was only posing and would get up and lend a hand. But she really was tuned out.

Wendy helped Rolf onto the couch and looked for blankets to cover him. His teeth were chattering and he moaned continually. Finally she covered as much of him as she could with her raincoat and the cover from the other couch. He stopped moaning when she held his hand, and again he wouldn't let her go.

When Jez came in, her face was flushed from running.

"Jez! Rolf's awfully sick. I don't know whether it's from his malaria or going out of his mind."

"You mean he's freaked out?"

"I don't know. He thought he was back in Vietnam in an air raid. He thought he was rescuing me from being shelled or something."

"Sure he's not just stoned? What was he on?"

"I don't know, Jez. I wasn't with him all evening. You're a nurse. Can't you tell?"

Jez bent over him, felt his forehead, and listened to his chattering teeth. "When in doubt try malaria pills, I guess."

"He said he kept them in his wardrobe—in his pants' pocket."

Jez loosened his belt, felt in his pocket, and found a little tin box of pills. She read the label and shrugged. "Hope these is them. At least it says how many and how often."

With some professional ability, she got him to loosen his hold on Wendy long enough for her to fetch a glass of water and to sit up enough to swallow the pills.

"Where does Rolf come from, Jez? This is all so ridiculous. I've known him a week, and I don't know his last name. He said he wanted to go home."

"He comes from Illinois somewhere. His last name is Snelson. His name's really Ralph—but he hates it. He got known as Rolf the Ready in Vietnam."

"Ready for what?"

"Ready to get out and go home," Rolf rasped. His teeth chattering intermittently.

"You mean you're ready to go back to Illinois? Can I call your home for you?" Wendy asked.

"Never. I'd die first," said Rolf. "No. The Ready was in Vietnam. Ready to get out of there."

"Why don't you just shut up and rest," said Jez curtly. "I'll put some water here to sip on."

She dragged the hassock to where he could reach his pills and the water. Wendy stopped the scraping record player.

"I'm tired tonight," Jez announced when she came out of the bathroom. "Oriana?"

Oriana lifted her head and smiled absently. "Yes?"

"We're going to sleep. I'll turn out the light. Don't disturb Rolf. He's sick."

"I don't need the light." Oriana put her head down

on her knees and shut them out of her sight and her mind. Jez wiggled onto the couch. Wendy was left with the floor. She was so exhausted it didn't keep her awake. But she didn't fall into any deep and dreamless sleep. Her dreams tormented her as she searched through them for Donald—missing the train she'd seen him board, the liner his taxi rushed him to, the helicopter that plucked him from its deck. Run as she would, she couldn't catch up to him anywhere.

And chasing behind her was Rolf. Time and again he nearly caught her, and she always knew he was close because even though he didn't talk, he made a ticking sound like the clock in the crocodile or like chattering teeth.

14

WENDY WOKE stiff and sore from her wretched night of bad dreams. Her arms were black and blue where Rolf's fingers had bruised her with his tremendous grip.

Oriana sang tunelessly from the kitchen. She'd just stirred herself some instant coffee, which momentarily had released a single burst of coffee aroma that encouraged Wendy to push herself off the floor.

"How's Rolf this morning?" Wendy asked, waiting for the kettle to boil again.

"I didn't look. Did you?"

"No. I can't unglue my eyes until I've had coffee. I just thought you'd been awake longer. You might have noticed."

"I'm not the nursely type." Oriana went on mouthing sounds in a distracting unmelodious way, as she cooled her coffee by stirring it around and around. It grated on Wendy's tired nerves.

"Is that a song? Or a kind of Pooh hum?"

"A Pooh hum?"

"You know. Winnie-the-Pooh. He hummed."

"So you were subjected to Pooh, too."

"I wasn't subjected. I loved him. We used to play

Winnie-the-Pooh out in our apple-jungle. Annetta always wanted to be Eeyore."

"If I ever had a child, and I may well not," said Oriana, "I shan't smother him with Pooh. Pooh is a fuzzy, false security blanket."

Wendy opened her mouth to protest, when Oriana went on. "I was saying 'Om' the way it should be said to open the mind. You know—the 'Awww' way in the back of the open throat and the 'mmmmmmmm' tickling behind your teeth. Vibrating."

"I always thought you just kind of swallowed the Om, like taking a bite of air."

"You know, you have an eager mind, Wendy. With the right tutor, or even your own guru, the right one for you, you probably could learn to have a very happy life. But it takes learning and practice."

"What? To turn on?"

"Anyone can turn on and get something out of it. I'm talking about getting the most out of it. Being the ultimate—a really consciously expanded being."

"Do you feel you are?"

"Of course. I'm calm, confident, and happy."

That sounds just like a deodorant ad! thought Wendy, and she looked to see if Oriana were being humorous. She wasn't. Wendy realized Oriana was never humorous—always serious. Wendy also realized the sink was full of garbage from the night before—potato peels, pea pods, discarded lettuce leaves, tea bags, and bread heels. She piled it into a paper bag and found the wastebasket under the sink ripening with another garbage bag full of chicken carcass and a suspicion of curry.

"Ugh. I'll take those out. Where does the garbage go?"

"All the way down to the cellar and out the back door. There's a big trash can out there. A garbage pail is beside it."

Wendy finished her coffee, grabbed the garbage,

and descended the two flights of stairs. At the back of the dim hall, she found the cellar stairs.

It seemed to be pitch dark below, and she felt around for a light switch. When she couldn't find one, she went down cautiously one step at a time.

Suddenly a voice from the top of the stairs called, "Wait right there," and a click switched on one dim bulb below. She was so startled she nearly dropped the garbage, and when she looked up, she was blinded by a flashlight shining in her eyes. She looked away and down, and when her eyes stopped dazzling, she saw someone lying on the floor at the foot of the stairs.

"She's all right, officer," the first voice said. "She lives in the flat above me. Wendy, come back up out of the way."

"Is someone hurt?" Wendy asked, and then realizing she was indeed in the way, she hurried up and saw Allan Westbox in the hall with two police officers, who quickly went down the stairs.

"I don't think anyone's hurt. But when I went down to the cellar this morning, I found some kids sleeping there. I don't know how they got in. So I called the police."

"You didn't just wake them up and warn them and tell them to beat it quick?"

"No. I didn't. It happened a couple of times in May before I went away. Just one or two kids, and I warned them then. But—look—this is just too much."

There was some scuffling below and voices raised as the police woke the crowd up. Wendy saw now that the front door was open, and two more policemen stood there, while a patrol wagon was outside.

One by one, kids, blinking and sometimes bewildered, were marched up the stairs and out to the wagon. Allan stood counting. When he got to thirteen, he said, "I don't believe it. Did you ever see the end of the play, *Arsenic and Old Lace*, when all the bodies come up from the cellar! It's just like that. Only more so."

Wendy gave a cry when she saw the fifteenth. It was Donald. She put down the garbage and ran to him. He looked terribly sleepy and very tired. "Oh, Wendy!" he whispered and put his arms around her and dropped his head on her shoulder. "Where have you been? I lost you—"

"Come on, there," said a policeman from the doorway. "We're providing free transportation. Come have a ride, fellow." The policeman stepped over and took Donald's arm. But he was kindly, and he didn't jerk at him. He just pulled firmly.

"Wendy—I'm going to jail!" Donald was suddenly panicked. "I can't. I can't! Please call my family. Tell them to come get me out."

The officer handed Donald on down the front steps. "Good idea if his family came and got him."

"Is that true?" Wendy asked. "Will you really put these kids in jail for just sleeping in a cellar?"

"They'll be booked and charged with trespassing and vagrancy. But from then on it's a court procedure. They won't be jailed right now anyway."

"Donald—" Wendy ran down the steps and yelled into the wagon. "They won't keep you after you're charged. So come back here."

The police brought out the last of the kids, a fragile, long-haired, long-legged blond girl who looked about fourteen. She was frightened and crying gustily. A policeman picked her up as she couldn't seem to walk and held her as if she were a baby, patting her shoulder. He looked so sadly at her, and there was nothing hard in his face—just a kind of appalled bewilderment.

He put her gently into the wagon and locked the doors. "I'll bet she's starving," he said. "She's skin and bones. Can you believe it. Twenty-two kids sleeping in that filthy place. That girl looks so much like my daughter Bonnie, I can't stand it."

The wagon drove quietly out of Sage Lane, and Wendy sat on the top step, feeling as though her legs

had given way. *Poor Donald.* If she'd only known he
was in the cellar! If only she'd gotten down there and
found him before that square, sanctimonious Allan
Westbox called the police.

"Did you know one of those kids?" Allan asked, coming out and sitting beside her.

"Yes. I just wish I'd found him in time to rescue him.
He was so frightened at being hauled off to jail, and he
wants me to call his family. And that means he's *really*
frightened. What did you do it for!"

"I don't enjoy making waves," Allan said soberly.
"But come down and look at that cellar. I'll show you
why I phoned the cops."

Reluctantly Wendy followed him. Allan very kindly
picked up her garbage bags and hurried ahead of her.
He had dumped them outside by the time she got down
the stairs. The floor and the walls were of cracked,
damp cement, and the smell was foul, as a bucket in a
corner had been used as a toilet. She saw well-gnawed
chicken bones and apple cores and orange peels also
in the corner.

"Did you ever read about the Black Hole of Cal-
cutta? See the size of this storage room? It doesn't even
run under the whole building. The furnace and boilers
take up the rest of the space behind that wood parti-
tion. I don't see how twenty-two kids could find room
to squat here overnight, let alone lie down and sleep.
And look over there. See that big rat hole? Some of
those kids were in such a state of exhaustion or stupor
that they wouldn't have felt a rat running around till
it bit them. I've lived in this building eight years, and
I've never seen anything like this spring and summer
for trespassing and burglaries. At first, Wendy, I was
tolerant. I've tried to help with handouts, no lectures,
and by ignoring things. But it's all out of control now.
And when public safety and numbers of people are
concerned, then it's time to stop ignoring the problems
and do something. Whether you think I'm right or

wrong by handling it that way. At least I'll bet those kids get to use a john and can wash up at the precinct station—if they want to."

She followed him up the stairs, still feeling shocked.

"You want to come along to the station with me? The police told me I have to make an affidavit or swear to a report or give a statement or something. You can see due process at work."

"No. I'll wait till Donald comes back here, and then I'll help him call his family. He may need some money, so I'll have to ask for that emergency fund after all."

"It's supposed to be for your use. Not to use on someone else."

"If I use it for Donald, it will still be for me."

"What's his name?"

"Donald Milner."

"I'll look him up and bring him back here if I can."

"Thanks."

"I can see I'm not going to get to work very fast today." He rushed off, kindly, concerned, and greatly irritated all at once.

Wendy found Jez and Oriana talking with Rolf, who looked much better. He was sitting up, sipping some lukewarm tea.

"What was all the commotion?" asked Jez. "I looked over the banisters until I saw it was fuzz. If it was a raid on a party in the first-floor apartment, it was sure a quiet party. I didn't hear anything all night."

"Neither did I," said Wendy. "I wonder if they all came in at once or a few at a time. There were twenty-two kids in the cellar. Including Donald."

"Wow! I suppose with Nell carted off last night he had to find a place to sleep for himself."

"He's coming back here. Do you mind, Oriana, if Donald stays with us?"

"Suit yourself," said Oriana.

"I mind," said Rolf. "Nell will mind. But you couldn't care less, right?"

Wendy nodded unhappily. Instead of being light-hearted and joyous, this tangle with love seemed to be the heaviest, most melancholy feeling she had ever suffered.

"Ha-ha on me," said Rolf. "Well, back to the hasheesh."

"Oh, stop it!" Wendy said impatiently. "Don't blame me for what you were doing before you even met me."

"I don't. I blame it on the war of liberation and justice we are so honorably fighting in Vietnam. You know that now."

"I know," Wendy told him. "I'm so sorry. About everything."

"Time for your pills," Jez announced, rattling his tin of antimalaria pills.

"Rot!" Rolf growled, and pulling the hassock to the window, rolled a cigarette. But ten minutes later he was back on the couch, shivering and shaking, and telling Jez to get him a glass of water and give him the pills after all.

Impatiently Wendy waited for Allan Westbox to return with Donald. It was a long morning. She played everything she could think of on her lute, argued with Jez, spooned tea into Rolf, and finally learned some premeditation exercises from Oriana.

"You mustn't be so tense," Oriana told her.

"This is pulling my muscles in a pretty tense way."

"Then you aren't doing it right." Oriana demonstrated again, and just as Wendy began to feel her muscles and her mind calming down, Allan knocked and came in.

Wendy leaped up. "Where's Donald!"

"He's in the hospital."

"What did they do to him!"

"Nothing. Look, Wendy. No one did anything to him. After he'd been booked or whatever they call it, he was released on his own word. He's supposed to go to court in about ten days. Anyway, I spoke to him and told him

I was just waiting to read over the complaint they'd typed up, and sign it, and then I'd walk back here with him. He agreed, and stood there with me. But he began sort of gulping and couldn't seem to get his breath, and then he just collapsed. All of a sudden, like a fan folding up. So they took him to Emergency at Boston City Hospital. I went along, Wendy, but all I could do was say his name was Donald Milner. And I'd try to find out more about him from you."

"I don't know any more. Do you?" She turned to the others. They couldn't help.

"I'll go find that Help Haven place. Donald said there was a letter posted there from his parents. If I can just remember where that place was."

"I'll take you in a taxi on my way to work," Allan said. "My boss is going to think I'm still away if I don't check in soon."

They couldn't find Help Haven in the phone book, but a policeman on Charles Street gave them the address. Luckily a cab came along. Allan insisted she take the ten dollars from Peter. "I'm sorry I haven't time to keep on helping you right now."

"That's all right. Thanks for all you've done—I think."

"I had to help you, if I could, because you thought this morning I was the enemy!"

Wendy entered the store and saw that bulletin boards covered both side walls, and each board was pinned full of messages. She started systematically scanning each one. There were several Donalds on the left-hand wall, but no message from the parents of Donald Milner. As she turned to the right side of the room, her neck ached and her eyes felt squinty and she had a kink in her back from stooping to read the bottom row. There were ten or twelve kids in the room, but only one man sat at a table in the back. He was talking to some parents who sat there, frown-faced and white-knuckled.

By the time Wendy came to the end of the second

wall and found no reference to Donald, she was panicky. She saw the man at the table was free, and she slid into the chair near him.

"What do you do with messages you take down?"

"If a situation is solved and parent and runaway are in contact again, we don't keep it. But all the current stuff is there. What are you looking for? A message from your parents and you don't see one?"

"It's not for me. It's for a Donald Milner. It's from his parents. He told me he'd been in here and read it once or twice—but he never spoke to anyone about it, I guess, or said he was Donald Milner. So it should still be there. It isn't, unless my eyes fooled me after a while."

The man took a notebook from a drawer. It was filled with names and dates. He looked under "M."

"You're sure it's Milner? Could it be Miller? Or Ronald instead of Donald?"

Wendy shook her head.

He flipped pages and compared lists of names. "We keep a cross-reference of every incoming request from parents for information, and the date when a message is posted. And an alphabetic list of missing kids. We've never had a Donald Milner reported to us nor a message posted for him nor a request from his parents for information. Maybe he'd got our place mixed up with some others. There's three private organizations like this in the greater Boston area. And most of the police precinct stations have lists."

"But we walked by *this* place, and he stopped and pointed it out to me and said it was here."

"Why doesn't he come in now?"

"He's in the hospital. He—collapsed."

"I see. Let me just make some phone calls for you. You look pretty beat to run around from one spot to another."

He spent a half hour thoroughly and carefully checking all the angles. No one in the Boston area had any messages from the parents of a Donald Milner.

"I'm sorry, dear," he said. "But you give me your phone number, and I can at least let you know if anything turns up."

She gave him Allan Westbox's name and address, and the man looked up the number and wrote it down. She started wearily home on foot, retracing the route she and Donald had taken along the river.

Turning into Charles Street, Wendy stopped by a bookstore window. She didn't really know what she was doing. She just stopped walking and couldn't seem to go on. She heard a familiar voice and at first didn't recognize Nell, because the girl was wearing blue jeans and an old man's shirt instead of one of her costumes. But she was wearing Wendy's garnet-and-silver earrings.

"Nell!" Wendy grabbed her. "I thought you were in jail!"

"Oh, hi." Nell smiled at her. "I was. Just overnight though. Say, that was sweet of you to tell Donald you wanted me to have your earrings. I love them. I wear them all the time except when I'm begging. Then they look too rich. But let me tell you something. I'm not swapping any earrings for Donald. So don't think you can bribe me. Where is he?"

"He's in the hospital. Nell, where does his family live? Who are his parents? He told me to call them, and the place where there was supposed to be a message from them never even heard of a Donald Milner."

"His family! Oh, God! Is he back on that kick again!"

"What do you mean?"

"He doesn't have a family. He's an orphan."

"But—he told me—"

"I know. Every now and then he flips and goes right out of his tree and thinks his parents are looking for him. It makes him feel better, he says. But I know the real Donald, and I know the truth. He hasn't any parents, and he grew up in an orphanage out on the prairie somewhere. And there's nothing you or anyone else can do to fix that."

15

"You mean Donald hasn't any mother!" Wendy was so shocked she whispered it.

"That's what I said. I know it sounds too much like an old-fashioned melodrama, but he really was abandoned at a Catholic orphanage when he was a few days old. He was brought up by priests, an order that originated in France. He learned French and Latin right along with English—just from listening, I guess. He's quite brilliant."

"He must be. He spoke French as if he'd lived over there. I thought he was even ex-jet set and had traveled all over."

"He's traveled all the way from Nebraska to Cambridge. He was a freshman at Harvard—on a full scholarship—when I met him this spring. He told me all about himself. How he grew up and was taught by the fathers in this prairie-town orphanage. He seemed quite calm about it. But after he had some bad trips and freaked out five or six times, he had a really bad trip and something happened. He insisted his mother and father were looking for him. He wouldn't admit he never even knew who his parents were. It got scary, because he's so weird now about it. It's like he's lost his mind."

"That wouldn't happen to Donald. It couldn't. He's not crazy."

"Of course he's not crazy. Just freaking out doesn't mean he's crazy."

"But they want to know about his relatives at the hospital. Will you go with me, Nell, and tell them? To Boston City Hospital?"

Nell plucked at Wendy's arm. "You didn't tell me what's wrong!"

"He collapsed. After the police picked him up."

"Could be shock then. After he dropped out at Harvard, he was scared of the police picking him up and sending him back to the orphanage or to a detention home or something. He can't seem to take care of himself any more. He just wanders. That's why I take care of him. I didn't know when he wandered off with you, whether you'd take care of him or not. I was frantic."

Wendy had been half walking and half running along Charles Street, with Nell two steps behind. But Wendy suddenly realized she didn't know where the hospital was. "Do you know how to get there, Nell?"

"Of course. I'm a graduate."

"You're a nurse, too? Like Jez?"

"You are really unreal, Wendy! You couldn't even cope with survival in our world yourself for one week. I'm a graduate of their hepatitis ward. I spent a month there last winter. Follow me."

Now that Nell knew she was on her way to Donald, she hiked through the streets at a furious pace, jaywalking through shrieking traffic without fear of car or cop.

The huge hospital had many different buildings and sections, but they finally were directed to the office which coped with records for the Emergency-Room patients. The woman at the desk had a form with the name Donald Milner written on it and nothing else.

Nell did her best with her scattered hearsay information, but the woman kept shaking her head at the number of questions that couldn't be answered. No birth date, although Nell said he said he was eighteen. No next of kin. No one to send bills to or give permission to operate. No medical history data. It still came down pretty much to just his name, Donald Milner. The woman sighed. "I'll have to speak with someone who is a case worker connected with the hospital and see what to do about this. Would you girls wait a few more minutes? There might be more questions—if anyone can answer them." She busied herself with the phone.

Nell and Wendy rested on a bench. "Nell—what if Donald isn't even Donald? I mean, does he *know* that was his name? Was it pinned on a blanket or something? Or did the fathers make up a name and give it to him?"

"They gave it to him. Of course it's the whole bit—Donald Xavier Milner."

"So he doesn't know who he really is—and he never will." Wendy wondered how the fact of never knowing who you really are would be to live with. She suspected that no matter how often you told yourself it wasn't all important, that you could live with it and overcome it, it was always inside, a built-in thorn, forever pricking.

In five minutes a brisk young woman in street clothes and horn-rimmed glasses asked the girls to step into her office. "I'm sort of Mrs. Follow-Up," she explained. "We do everything we can, in a situation like this boy's, to find the right authority to help him. Now—it takes time and red tape. I'll call Harvard and check their records and see what orphanage he came from. We'll do everything we can to see he's taken care of."

"Does he have to stay here?" asked Nell. "I mean—I thought he just kind of passed out and—"

The woman looked at the record blank. "He was admitted in a state of shock. That can have physical causes. Or mental causes. Or both. I'm sure he won't be released for several days."

"Can we see him? Or talk to his doctor?" Wendy asked.

The woman picked up the phone and made a call. "He's now in a ward bed, and it's not advisable for him to see anyone. Not today. His doctor says he'll know more tomorrow. You girls can phone me about one o'clock tomorrow afternoon, and I'll tell you if you can see him during visiting hours. And you can tell me if you've remembered anything more about him that would help. Here's my name and the phone extension number."

When Wendy and Nell walked out, neither of them felt like talking. Each was absorbed in her own thoughts about Donald. But Nell followed Wendy across the city and back to Sage Lane. She followed Wendy right up the stairs and into Oriana's apartment, where she sat on a couch, smoking and frowning—while Wendy told the others about Donald.

Suddenly Nell interrupted. "I don't know why you're spreading the news about Donald's being an orphan. He wouldn't like it."

"No one's going to greet him as 'Hi, there, Orphan.' Or 'Hey, look at the Great Unknown!'" Jez said.

"It all sounds kind of tittle-tattley," Nell said huffily. "If nobody knows, it's easier for him to keep his illusions."

"But isn't that the trouble?" asked Wendy. "Maybe he shouldn't keep his illusions, if they're what's troubling him."

Nell shrugged and glowered. Wendy grew very restless and took out her lute and sat in a corner playing it. Rolf still lay on the couch. He'd gone from shivering and needing layers of clothing to sweating all the time. But he insisted he was better and tomorrow he'd be fine. Oriana announced that anyone who was hungry could make a sandwich. Nell promptly did, which annoyed Jez and Wendy. It annoyed Wendy even more when Nell put a record on and drowned out the lute with the Rolling Stones at full roll.

Wendy wasn't hungry. She stamped out of the apartment and banged on Allan Westbox's door. But he wasn't in. Nor was Zack. She hadn't seen him since Peter left.

She wandered as far as the Common where she leaned against a tree and listened and looked and wished the magic feeling she'd had the night Donald gave her the pink feather flower to hold would come back. But it didn't. She stood there, unfeeling, unreal in the midst of a real scene that didn't touch her. A long time went by, during which she felt quite empty, as if she knew she existed, but she didn't seem really to care.

Finally she could see the sides drawing up for another skirmish at the curfew—police closing in, spectators gathering, and hippies and teen-agers in the middle. She couldn't bear being caught up in it again, so she walked past the Frog Pond and crossed Beacon Street and went through the quiet streets at the top of the Hill. When the sirens began screaming, it was remote, but the sounds made her shiver.

At Sage Lane she found the front door locked. With Allan Westbox in residence again things were different. Wendy rang the bell for Oriana's flat and after five long, loud rings, the door buzzed, and she could open it. She found it was Rolf who'd gotten up to let her in. The girls were asleep.

"Don't you want the couch, Wendy?" he asked. "I'm a lot more used to the floor than you are."

"No. I'm used to it myself now."

"But I want to talk to you. Come listen. Please."

Rolf sounded lonely, and Wendy felt the same way, although she didn't want to admit it. So she sat on the floor by the couch and listened, and Rolf talked for an hour, while she half dozed and half answered and gave him glasses of cold water when he asked for them. All the time there was a question chewing away at Wendy. *What am I doing here? What am I proving to myself? Why do I expect something special, something more from all these people? Why can't I find it? Am I too hung-up to enjoy this? What's wrong with me?*

What's wrong with you, Wendy? Maybe it's your breath. The commercial words appeared in her brain as automatically as she could hear them on television. *Well, that world is pretty unreal, too,* Wendy realized. *What's real? What's unreal? And how do I find out?*

Rolf was still talking when Wendy fell asleep.

The next day was one long wait. Nell made no move to go off about her own affairs. Instead she picked arguments. She argued with Oriana about the poster on the wall, with Jez about where a certain street was in the Village, and with Rolf about the cheapness of spending the winter in Mexico as against California. But she avoided speaking to Wendy at all.

Finally Oriana took some money out of the sugar bowl, and Jez went with her. What they were shopping for, Wendy wasn't quite sure. Wendy wanted to leave, too—to walk by the river or read on the Common. Anywhere to have some peace. Even though she often felt oddly alone while the others were around her, it wasn't the same as being by herself. She thought more than once of the tree hut at Meridian Farm. The boys hadn't used it as much last summer, and Wendy often hid there and read or drew for undisturbed hours.

"You know what!" Wendy said in complete exasperation. "We're supposed to phone that woman at one o'clock—and there isn't a working clock or watch in this whole apartment. Or a radio. Or a telephone. No one ever knows what time it is. And this time it matters."

"Go out and ask someone," said Nell. "People on the street don't mind being asked for the time or a match. They just get stuffy about being asked for cigarettes or money."

Wendy looked glumly at Nell. Until they knew about Donald, she was determined not to fight with her—verbally or physically. But seeing her earrings flaunted by Nell's ears was becoming more and more of a provocation every minute. She knew she never, never would have offered them to Nell if she knew what she was doing. And she wanted them back.

"Nell, did you come over to Cambridge Sunday night and find Donald and me at the apartment of some guy named Charlie?"

"Sure. I began to think of the places Donald might go. And when he wasn't at other places, I went there. And were you stoned!"

"I was?"

"Can't you remember?"

"Quite honestly, no. I certainly don't remember offering you those earrings. I'd never have done it in my right mind."

"Then I guess there's a lot you don't remember."

"Could be." Wendy's voice shrank to a mumble. "It all seemed unreal."

"Do you want me to give you a play-by-play description?"

Wendy stood there uncomfortably, trying to make up her mind if she wanted Nell to tell her or not. Then just as she wondered if Nell's idea of what was real and what wasn't was any clearer than hers at the time, or if Nell would just be telling her own angles or illusions, there was a knock on the door. Peter and Zack walked in.

Wendy was relieved to see them, but she didn't feel like giving them a big greeting.

"Good! You're still here, Wendy," Peter said. "Zack and I want to talk to you. Come on downstairs."

They looked more dressed up than usual, and Peter explained they'd just come up from New York on the shuttle. Wendy found that Allan Westbox was at work. Zack kicked off his shoes, pulled off his socks, ripped off his tie and said, "Ugh. There's one revolt I'm with all the way."

Peter grinned, took off his tie, and offered Wendy a Coke, which she accepted greedily.

"Now, I owe you an explanation. And an apology for taking advantage of you."

"You mean you really did consider me an 'innocent bird'? I heard you say it on the phone."

"I'm sorry you overheard that, Wendy, but like it or not, you were absolutely the most perfect innocent bird ever, and I thought you were the answer to my search. You see, I do have a job. I am helping to make a study for a foundation—one of the big foundations that puts hundreds of thousands of dollars into projects to better mankind. But that foundation is run by a very hard-nosed board of directors, who want to make sure the project is needed and that it's worthwhile. I believe the project is vital, as do the doctors and the sociology and psychology professors who initiated the idea. You see, I'm working for my master's degree in a combination of sociology and related psychology, and Professor Zim, who is my advisor, has some great ideas to do with the project. He asked me to help him document stuff this summer which will help him to persuade the directors of the foundation to finance the project."

"But if you're studying for your master's, what was all that line about quitting a job on Wall Street? That phone call sounded phony—the more I think about it. But I swallowed it, didn't I?"

"Actually, I was talking to Professor Zim. He knew at once the call was a put-on and something I needed to do so you'd trust me. So he was giving me some appropriate jazz in return. But he did get the message. Now—about this project. If it is worked out right, it could do two things. First, it could help kids who are struggling to find their own identity in the midst of all our drastic problems today. It would help them understand themselves in relation to life and society. And second, it could help society to understand the kids and their drastic problems. That's the oversimplification of the year, to state the project in those terms. But that's the purpose of it."

"Why couldn't the directors of this foundation go along with it then? It sounds real do-goody."

"I think that's why they are suspicious. There's lots of do-goody agencies that run with varying degrees of success. But this project would have to be a study in great depth to evaluate the basic causes of the problems first, and then how to treat the causes, or the do-goody part, would come second."

"I don't see how that could remotely have anything to do with me."

"Because I had what I thought was a bright idea. Most of these gentlemen on the board are highly qualified in their fields—business, science, or education. They're all successful and high-powered. Most are fathers and some are grandfathers. Some of them have intellectual understanding of the problems. They can theorize and grasp all kinds of mathematical and scientific projections on charts and maps. Some of the men would vote funds for the project on theoretical understanding alone. But they'd expect in a certain amount of time to see results that could be plotted on charts and graphs. No results. End of funds. Follow me?"

"I think so."

"With these men there would be more than just a generation gap or two. There would also be a tremendous sociological and psychological gap. And they wouldn't fight for that project and see it through no matter how long or how much money it took, just on intellectual understanding, with these big gaps in their background. We want them to see the problems on a one-to-one basis, through emotional involvement. So they'd not only vote for the project but be hooked on it. It would be a consuming interest to them. Conviction is as important as money, maybe more so. Anyway—my idea was to find a young girl from a background they knew and could understand because they could relate to it. You know—the whole bit—well-brought-up family, good schools, privileged, if you like, environment. Relative affluence. I wanted to find a girl of that background and document by pictures and taped conversations what happened to her when she tried out the hippie life. How she reacted physically and mentally, what risks she took knowingly or unknowingly, and what the consequences were. That day you walked in I was on my way to the Village to hang around and see if I could pick up just such a girl—someone just arriving, looking for the action. I could hardly believe it when you sat there saying you didn't want to go home."

"I talked myself into this, didn't I?" Wendy murmured.

"When I found the girl, I was going to phone Zack to come to the Village, and we'd work as a team on the tapes and the pictures. But the big thing was—the girl couldn't be aware of it. If we told her, she'd be unnatural—acting or inhibited or concerned. You know."

"And that's why you wouldn't tell me what you were doing?"

"Right. But even though you were the perfect girl, you ruined the documenting."

"Why?"

"Because I got concerned. Knowing you were a friend of my sister and then talking to your father on the phone, I felt a responsibility for you that otherwise wouldn't have gotten in my way. I suddenly didn't feel right about just letting you beat your way into the Village and take all the risks of getting mixed up with hard-line dope addicts and the rapists and perverts that girls can unknowingly fall victim to in a very short time. The Village can be an ugly scene. So I did phone Zack, but he suggested bringing you to Boston. Actually Boston is supposed to be the big scene this summer, so it did make some sense. And Professor Zim is here, conducting his research on the Common and other likely spots. And I knew Oriana was living upstairs. So it all seemed to work together. I thought Oriana would be enough of a hippie to fascinate you, but I'd be pretty sure you wouldn't come to any serious harm."

"That's for sure!" Wendy snapped. "You might as well have run a test in a laboratory. I've been just a sort of controlled experiment. Right?"

"Fortunately for you, yes. Unfortunately for me, yes. You make an interesting case study. But not a vital one. I don't think I can get a grip on that board of directors with the Story of Wendy A."

"You aren't going to use the Story of Wendy A." Wendy banged her fist onto the coffee table so hard that her glass of Coke bounced. She was almost as mad as when she first saw the table covered with her pictures and their captions.

"Not as Wendy A. No!" Peter said hastily. "We'll change the name to protect the innocent."

"You aren't going to use that material under any name! Who do you think you are, to spy on a girl living her private life? Or to set her up for any experiment in living, controlled or otherwise, and then use the consequences for your own benefit."

"But it's not for my benefit," Peter argued. "It's for the general humanitarian good. It might even be for your own good."

"How? How can something be for my good when there's nothing bad? I am going *harmlessly* about my business, not hurting anyone, and I'm leading a *perfectly harmless life*. No one is hurting me. I may be smoking pot, but I can't see anything wrong with it. I can't see what's so wrong about the kids I'm with, just because they smoke pot."

"What about speed? What about acid? I understand there was a speedy little party upstairs over the weekend."

"I wasn't there."

"How about where you were?"

Wendy shrugged.

"Well," said Peter, watching her, "I hope you know where you're at, if you think there's nothing wrong with pot and speed. Because I don't agree with you. I told you I'd been the whole route and I have, including a very bad trip. That's why I feel so strongly about what I'm trying to do."

"I don't think drugs are the point. The main point is my right to lead my own life and that it is nothing to document. Nobody's going to document me so a foundation will vote a project to give lectures about drugs to kids who don't want the lecture."

Then Peter grew angry. "You sit down, Wendy A., and you listen. Let's get one thing straight. This isn't a lecture project. The idea behind this is a one-to-one relationship with a counselor—who is usually an ex-addict. Showing a kid, not telling him, how turning off drugs is going to make him more aware of life and the joys of being alive than any drug ever could. The project is to convince kids they can turn on without drugs. You know when you give up smoking tobacco you begin to taste things again and smell things again and breathe better and feel better. Well, it's more exciting to discover what your mind can find on its own than under the distortion of a drug. Or that you can discover meaningful relationships with people without the false stimulus of a drug."

"But you just can't go around telling people how to live."

"Now you're expressing the attitudes we need to study."

"Peter! I am not an exhibit. Go back to the Village and find some dumb girl who gets into real trouble—gets arrested or raped or murdered. Then you'll have a real case history for your directors to gloat over. I just don't think real life is like that. You're making it very unreal. Anyway, leave me and my friends alone."

Peter turned to Zack and shook his head. "Where have I heard all this before. 'Leave me and my friends alone.' Arrgh! Bletch! Zap! Scream!" He looked quite distraught. "It's all my fault. I should have turned you out of twelve-C that day to go your own way. To run back home or run into trouble on your own with no help from me. I'm sorry, Wendy. I almost started to persuade you to get off the train at Westerly on the way to Boston that night. But I didn't listen to myself hard enough. So—I'm sorry. Go your own way. Zack and I had about decided to shift back to the Village anyway to do another case history—one that would be more convincingly sordid. So I won't use the stuff about you, if you still object."

"I object."

"All right. That's it. But it's been nice knowing you. Can't we be friends anyway?"

"You really are a kook!" Wendy stared at him. She put her empty Coke glass down and stood up to go.

"Wait a minute," said Zack. "You're being rough on Peter. In fact, we both lost our scientific objectivity on this, once we got to know you. You've been a real hang-up—with our wanting the documentary to be a success —but not wanting anything to happen to you."

"Nothing has happened to me, thanks to you. Congratulate yourselves. I've stayed a plastic, pseudo-hippie just like the little girls who run in from Brookline and watch. Now—are you satisfied? Can I go on my merry way and get hurt all on my own without your help? You're so sure I'm going to."

"Can you look me in the eye, Wendy, and tell me you haven't changed one little bit?" Peter asked. "Because I won't believe it. You're no longer the girl you were on the train."

"If I have changed, it's none of your business, Peter. Besides, I'm the one who didn't make a vital case history for you after all, remember?" Wendy marched out and shut the door firmly behind her. Just as she was going to let go of the knob so it would latch she remembered something and opened the door again. "And I'll mail your ten dollars back to Apartment twelve-C. In September. When I get home."

"Forget it," Peter muttered crossly. "Forget the whole thing."

Upstairs, Wendy found only Rolf who was sleeping deeply and didn't wake up even when she kicked the hassock as enthusiastically as she wanted to kick Peter Banbury. She sat, elbows on the windowsill, head in hands, and stared out at Sage Lane. *I feel like a—like a rejected guinea pig!* was all she could think, and it was a very uncomfortable feeling. But when she calmed down and thought of Peter's quiet question, and the disquieting questions she'd asked herself in the last day or two, she knew she'd been unfair answering his questions, even though she felt absolutely right in not going along with his project.

I just want to be left alone, Wendy decided. *But with Donald. Just as Oriana wants to be left to her own way of life with William. And Jez wants to—what? What did Jez want?* Wendy had the feeling Jez lived in a mirror that reflected Oriana rather than herself. And Rolf? He was retreating, too. Not as badly as Donald, but still retreating.

Suddenly Wendy wondered where Nell was. It must be after one o'clock, and she realized that Nell had sneaked off to see Donald without her.

Furiously Wendy ran out and headed toward the hospital.

16

IT WAS TWO-THIRTY when Wendy found that there was some confusion over Donald Milner's whereabouts. He was no longer listed as a patient in the ward where he had been placed the day before. The girl at the reception desk, a bewildered vacation replacement learning her way through her hectic first day, thought his records had gone to the case worker's office. But when Wendy got there, Mrs. Follow-Up had gone, and no one could give Wendy any further information.

If I hadn't been down talking to Peter Banbury, Nell couldn't have gone off without me and sneaked Donald away somewhere. The thought haunted Wendy's mind as she walked slowly through the hot streets. *Peter Banbury has ruined my life.*

Wendy searched the whole route—the Public Garden, the Common, the river bank—anywhere she thought Nell and Donald might be sitting out the uncomfortable afternoon. It was still hazy in her mind what she intended to do when she found Donald. Put him on the spot by accusing him of abandoning her in Cambridge? Ask him what had happened to her there, when she didn't even want to hear it from Nell? Ask Nell to let her take care of Donald? Ask Donald to choose between them? It was all too fantastic to make any sense. But she couldn't seem to realize that. All she knew was that she ached to see Donald. She hated Peter Banbury. And she thought Peter, with his reformed, smug, square attitude about drugs was more repressively harmful to society at large than drugs. *The worst thing in the world is to* use *someone. And Peter was using me. He's despicable!*

She returned dejectedly to the apartment, intending to scout Charles Street again late in the day when Nell usually did her panhandling.

Oriana and Jez were happily squeezing rather over-ripe limes to make a big pitcher of fresh fruit juice for Rolf. On the floor there was a large round tray full of fruit, all just a little past its prime, which they had washed and shined and arranged in an eye-filling pyramid.

"We've been to the fruit market," Jez announced. "If you hit it right, you can buy a week's supply cheap."

"It looks too lovely to eat now," said Oriana. She pulled her "Do Not Sell" box from under the couch and took out a large pad of good watercolor paper and a well-used box of paints. Wendy saw that the sable brushes were in excellent condition. Oriana probably felt about her paints and brushes the way Wendy did about her lute.

Oriana laughed at the dark purple walls and the tiny windows. "Not very light-making in here, is it!" She pulled the tray nearer the front window and put it up on the hassock to give herself more of an eye-level view as she sat on the floor. She slightly rearranged the fruit.

"Jez, some mood music, please. Anything but Shankar. He's too diverting. Maybe some Satie."

Jez dug in the records and found Satie. But Oriana worked so deftly and with such concentration that Wendy wondered if she even heard the music. It didn't even seem to bother her that Rolf and Jez and Wendy all sat and watched.

Wendy saw that Oriana wasn't just dubbing around. The technique was professional, and the approach, neither realistic nor completely abstract, had style and conviction. She was working, also, with acrylic paint which took experience to handle well.

"She's so good! Why doesn't she paint more often?" Wendy asked Jez.

"I heard that," Oriana said, pausing to wash out a brush. "I think you should only paint when you see something to say. And things just don't strike me that intensely very often. The Art Students' League when I was there was just cluttered with people painting *stuff*. And selling it. But what did it mean—to them or anyone else?"

In half an hour more, she'd finished. She carefully picked up her paints and put them away. The paper lay drying on the floor—an intense, black-outlined, stained-glass impression of shapes and colors of fruit, against, of course, a deep purple background. It was unusual and rather disturbing.

"What's the matter, Wendy?" Jez asked. "If it's so good, don't you like it?"

"I think it's amazingly good. But it makes me realize how differently I see and how differently I'd paint it."

"So?" Oriana asked. "Should we all see and paint alike? 'Now children, we will all draw a tree and a sun and a mother and child out for a walk. The tree will be green and the sun is yellow and the mother is pretty and the child is white.' First grade. First lesson. Amen." She finished with an ugly word which Wendy had already realized was Oriana's punctuation, like "stop" in a telegram. But it always sounded displaced from her beautifully formed lips. Oriana was one of the most surprising and puzzling people Wendy had ever known. *She doesn't add up*, Wendy thought. *And she doesn't make sense to me. But that's like our seeing the fruit and painting it in different ways, I guess. I'm see-*

ing her one way and she sees herself another. And I like her, so what does it all matter anyway?

"I'm going out and look for Nell again," Wendy told them. "If she should come up here, by any chance, please make her wait for me!"

After another two-hour search, Wendy decided Nell was deliberately avoiding her. Since she didn't know any of the places where Nell and Donald put themselves up, except for Charlie's in Cambridge on weekends only when his aunt was away, she stumbled back to Sage Lane so exhausted that she wanted to fling herself onto a couch and cry and cry.

But Oriana was sitting on one couch, opposite her meditating poster, and oblivious of anything around her. Rolf lounged on the other couch. He looked at Wendy and promptly poured out the lukewarm limeade left in the pitcher for her. "Didn't you see them anywhere?"

"Not a trace."

"Wendy, let me tell you a truth. You're better off without Donald. He is the helpless sort who triggers the mother in half the girls on Charles Street. You can take that statement either way you see fit. But it's a well-known fact. You're not the first and you won't be the last. Nell is just the most aggressive and the most persistent. And Donald's wide-eyed charm has been as well used as Nell's ability to panhandle. You've been had. All you can do is forget it and get over it. I'm sorry you got hurt."

"What makes you think I'm hurt!"

"Because you write your woes unconsciously all over your face, and I'm not blind."

"I wish I had an iron face!" Wendy said furiously.

Rolf laughed. Then he stood up and stretched. "Ha! That feels good. See? I'm all better. Want to come for a walk?"

"Are you mad? My feet are swollen. I've walked miles over hot sidewalks today. But keep an eye out for

Nell, will you? Even if I can't get Donald back, I want my earrings."

Rolf laughed again. He suddenly pulled her close and hugged her, rather gently for him, and kissed her cheek. "Forget Donald?" he whispered hopefully. "I'll help you forget."

"Oh, Rolf!" Wendy tried wriggling away from him. "I don't want to talk about it. Please."

"All right." But he gave her a hard kiss on the mouth before he let her go. "I'll be back."

Wendy dropped onto the couch. It felt so good just to lie there with her eyes closed. She heard Jez come out of the bathroom and ask Rolf to wait for her. She needed to find the same guy Rolf did, so they might as well go along together.

"Slip the latch on the door, will you, Rolf? I've lost the key again, and we don't want to disturb Oriana with the bell if we don't have to."

Wendy fell asleep before their footsteps echoed down the stairs.

Suddenly she was awakened by someone pulling at her wrist and trying to haul her off the couch onto her feet.

"Get up! Get up and you come with me!"

Wendy had been so deeply asleep that she was disoriented. At first she wasn't sure it really was Nell leaning over her and twisting her arm. But it was—a stern, unsmiling, grim-faced Nell.

"Oh, Nell!" Wendy gasped. "I've been looking everywhere for you. How's Donald? Where is he?"

"Just you come with me." Nell kept tugging at her.

Wendy finally unglued her eyes and felt steady enough to stand. "All right. Don't pull at me. I'm coming." But when she took a really good look at Nell, Wendy was frightened. Nell somehow didn't seem to be acting normally.

"Oriana?" Wendy stooped down into what she hoped was Oriana's line of sight as she meditated, unmov-

ingly, unblinkingly. "Oriana, will you tell Rolf or Jez
when they come back that I've gone off with Nell—to
see Donald?"

Oriana didn't respond. Wendy was cross. She
couldn't help wondering if it was for real—that Oriana
really didn't hear and see what went on around her. Or
she did, but she wouldn't acknowledge it.

Nell impatiently started out the door, and Wendy
followed. But she paused on the second-floor landing.
"Nell—does Donald need any money—or any help? I
just might be able to get someone who could help him."

"I'm going to help him," Nell said grimly. "Hurry up."

Nell walked so fast down the Hill that her bell-bottoms made a swishing noise. Wendy, wincing with
every step on her sore feet, kept up as best she could.
Nell seemed to be taking all the dark streets, and
Wendy was surprised to find how few people were
around. She wondered what time it was.

Finally Nell came out on Cambridge Street near the
pedestrian bridge across the traffic circle. It was a
strange confusion of city transportation, for an above-
ground subway station rose up in the midst of the circle
in a large tower, and the pedestrian bridge led through
the tower.

The sour-blue, high-intensity lights made the scene
lonely, eerie, and cold, despite the heat of the night and
the cars and trucks which shot down the main arteries
and into the circle, headlights blazing like furious
tigers' eyes. *Tiger, tiger, burning bright, in the forests
of the night,* went through Wendy's mind.

Wendy put her hand on the railing to help haul herself wearily up the stairs to the bridge. Suddenly Nell
whirled around and grabbed Wendy's hand in a painful grip, bending back one of her fingers. Wendy was
paralyzed with fear and pain. The car lights flashing
by were as wildly psychedelic as the lights at the pill
party. Wendy tried to back away and get down off the
stairs, but Nell was unexpectedly strong and clever.

She had only to twist Wendy's hand and push back her finger to make her move up a step and another step and another step.

"Go ahead!" Nell taunted her. "Yell! No one will hear you with the traffic." A subway train roared and shook into the station above them, and cars whooshed below. "And if they do, do you think anyone would help if you yelled 'help'? Not in this place. Not now."

They reached the top of the stairs, and Nell pulled Wendy along over the traffic circle.

"I want you to know what you did—that's what I want." Nell stopped, Wendy's hand still in a viselike grip of Nell's two hands. Nell managed to turn Wendy with her, so their backs were to people passing behind them on the narrow bridge. "You had Donald committed to an insane asylum. That's what you did."

"I—*what?*" If Nell hadn't been holding her so tight, Wendy might have fallen, she felt so faint at hearing such news. "I couldn't even find anyone this afternoon who knew where he'd gone! So how could I have sent him anywhere! You're crazy. Nell!"

"Oh, no. I'm not crazy. But they claim Donald is. Freaked right out of his mind. Permanently."

"Nell, you're hurting me. Just let go—so we can talk. I'm not going to run out on you and Donald. Not when I might be able to help." Desperately she wondered if Peter Banbury's professor made Donald his document, if that would arouse the right help and treatment for Donald.

"Help? You? You didn't help Donald escape from the police when he was picked up in the basement and that was what did it. He was so afraid that he schizo-ed right out of this world. They didn't even bother to keep him at City Hospital. They just shipped him right out to the State Hospital in Waltham this noontime. He'd been sent off already when I got there, because he'd gotten so violent during the night, and they didn't have any more room to keep another violent patient they said. They're full up."

"How did you find out all that? I couldn't find out anything."

"That woman we saw yesterday told me where he'd been transferred. So I hitched to Waltham. They finally let me see him, and he didn't know me. He didn't know me! He swore he'd never seen me before in his life. Then he wouldn't talk to me. He just sat there, muttering things that meant nothing to us. He tells them he's only five years old, and his mother and father are going to come and take him home." Nell began to cry. "This never would have happened if you had taken care of Donald. I hate you, Wendy—and I'm not going to let you get away with it, do you hear?"

The subway train roared off again with a thunder of sound, so Nell had to scream. But Wendy heard her. So did several people who were hurrying from the train and would scurry uneasily through the streets until they reached the hoped-for safety of their apartments. But even though they saw two girls, one of them screaming, no one stopped to see if anything was wrong.

Wendy made a sudden move and pulled free. She intended to rush back to the Hill side of the traffic circle, but Nell was in the way. So Wendy had to run toward the subway terminal. She was off in a flash, her leather sandals slipping on the concrete. Wendy hoped there would be a patrolman inside the small tower. But there wasn't. Just a man at the change booth who was so hardened to fights and people yelling and kids chasing that he looked up and didn't even blink when Wendy rushed through the doors and out onto the other wing of the bridge, with Nell cursing and reaching to try and grab Wendy's hair or sleeve.

Wendy found herself so scared she could barely breathe, but she could feel Nell only a step behind.

Then as she leaped down the iron stairway, Wendy's flat leather-soled sandals slipped and she fell. She plunged downward and felt her head bang on the edge of a step, and lights spun dizzily through her sight. Her ears buzzed and hummed. Then Nell tripped over her and her body thrust past, landing down on the stairs with a terrible thud, her weight nearly knocking out what breath Wendy had left. But Nell's head connected with a step with a horrid whack. Nell didn't move, and Wendy lay gasping for a few seconds. Then she tried to wiggle out from under Nell's weight. When she heard footsteps coming along the bridge to the stairs, she felt frantic. She didn't want anyone to see her in such a mess.

But the footsteps came onto the stairs and then, to her relief, she heard familiar voices. Jez and Rolf reached down to pull Nell out of the way and help Wendy up. All Wendy could do was hold onto Rolf, sag against him, and cry.

Jez, in some remnant of her nurse's training, was checking Nell for broken bones. Nell sat, groaning, on the stairs, and a large bruise already had egged up on her forehead. Jez waved her hand in front of Nell's staring eyes and got a hard-eyed response.

"Can you bend your neck?" Jez asked her.

Nell tried it and then stood up. Jez helped her down the stairs. "You ought to go over to Emergency at MGH, Nell. You might have a concussion."

"Do you think I'm out of my trees?" Nell said hoarsely. "You walk in there, and they put you down as crazy and ship you off for the rest of your life." The tears rolled down her face, but Wendy couldn't tell whether she was crying from pain or rage.

It must have been partly pain, as she cried out when she raised her hands and slipped the garnet and silver earrings out of her ears. She thrust them at Jez. "Give those back to that creepy girl, Wendy. I don't want them any more. She's brought nothing but trouble."

Jez caught the earrings as Nell suddenly darted into the street, despite the circling traffic. Brakes shrieked, and a taxi driver swore and just missed turning into another car. But Nell made it to the shadows of the center island and, in a lull of cars, to the river side of Charles Street.

Jez watched her limp off. "She ought to have gone to the hospital," she said again and shook her head. "How about you, Wendy? Are you hurt?"

"My knee is bleeding. But it's just a scrape I think. And my head aches. That's all."

"And you're shaking like you're the one with malaria. Come on, Rolf. Let's get her home."

Somehow they pushed and pulled Wendy back up the stairs, across the bridge and down, along Charles Street, up the Hill, and Rolf found strength to carry her up the two flights of stairs at Sage Lane.

Oriana was still meditating, but not so rigidly. When Rolf put Wendy down on the couch and Jez dashed to boil some water to wash out the dirty cut on her knee, Oriana snapped out of her remoteness.

"What happened!" she demanded.

"Jez and I went out to find our man for some stuff. And afterward Jez wanted some ZigZag papers. So we walked to that drugstore on the traffic circle. Just as we came out of the store, we saw Nell and Wendy, and Nell had some kind of hold on Wendy and forced her up on the bridge. What was she trying to do to you, Wendy? Kill you?"

17

"MAYBE NOT kill me." Wendy was too shocked still to believe that. "But do something to scare me or hurt me —that's for sure. She says I'm responsible for Donald being taken away from her and stuck out at a state hospital. He's really flipped, I guess. She blames me. Maybe it is all my fault, but I don't think so. I don't know."

Wendy would have howled again out of sheer misery, but Jez came with hot water and soap and a rough towel and began scrubbing out the grit embedded in the cut knee. It was a deeper cut than Wendy had realized.

"Yipe!" said Wendy. "That—hurts."

Rolf put an arm around her. "You should see what they use to scrub out wounds with in Vietnam. Wire brushes—they feel like. I swear they're wire brushes."

"I'm being as gentle as I can, Wendy. You know why I gave up nursing? Because I couldn't bear to hurt people. And you can't help it—moving them around—and they moan and cry. It was too much."

"I suppose you'd better get the dirt out. Wouldn't that be a way to go! Lockjaw from a dirty step in Boston."

"Maybe you ought to get a tetanus shot," Jez said.

"I had a booster last summer. Stepped on a rusty nail in the tree hut."

"A tree hut?"

Rolf got Wendy to tell them about the tree hut, while Jez finished scrubbing and found some Methiolate in the medicine cabinet and painted her knee bright red.

"There you are. But what's the matter with your finger, Wendy? It looks like a baseball bat."

"It's sprained, I guess. It didn't hurt until now—and all of a sudden, I can really feel it."

Jez provided ice cubes to numb the pain. Rolf rolled her a cigarette. "How about some grass?"

"Not if it just magnifies the pain, like it magnifies everything else!" Wendy shuddered. "I'll skip it for now."

Rolf shrugged and smoked it himself.

"We do have some aspirin." Oriana finally found it in the kitchen, and Wendy saw it was really aspirin.

Sitting down again Oriana said, "I was meditating on a decision tonight, and I've made it. I'd better tell you, because it will affect you, too. After all, we've been kind of a family for six months or so—Jez and Rolf, and sometimes William, and Robbie and Charlene, and some others who've already left Boston. Courtesy of dear old Dad's stuffy lawyer I've been able to provide a roof over our heads, and it's been my pleasure, kiddies. It was worth one hour of my time each month to sit there and listen to all that crap from Mr. Beasley and get the rent money just so I could use it in a way they'd hate. But somehow they've been checking up on me and found I wasn't doing any settlement or volunteer work. And Mr. Beasley also accused me of having quite a few 'people,' as he put it, living with me."

"Is that what you told him you were doing? Settlement work?" Jez admired Oriana's definition.

"Why not?" Oriana shrugged. "Isn't this a sort of settlement? Anyway, Mr. Beasley told me the other day

that Daddy was through paying my rent. It was a job
—or get out. I didn't tell you right away because I
wanted to think about it. We're paid up until next week
anyway. But I honestly can't see taking a job—much as
I like to have us together. I feel so much more at home
and happier than I ever did with my own family. But
I've had jobs before, and I just can't stick to them."

"I know what you mean," said Jez. "Boredom."

"So, I've decided to join William at the farm until the
winter comes. Then we'll probably go to Mexico. Anyway, I'm sorry. But that's it. There's room at the farm
if you don't mind that terrible, bleak, tree-filled country all around."

"And you're the one who doesn't like being out in the
country!" Jez said sympathetically.

"I know. I need crowds, cities, neon lights. Nature is
fine for a few days at a time, but that's all. However,
William and I make out together pretty well. We'll just
try being together all the time and see if it gets more
meaningful or less. So. Jez, you want to come?"

"I don't know. I'm not that keen on nature either. I
might just go back to Jersey and look up my friend. If
I can come and visit you once in a while. You're the
one close friend I've ever had, you know."

"I know," said Oriana, accepting the tribute but not
making anything out of it. "What about you, Rolf?"

"Oh, not to worry." Rolf looked undismayed. "It
really doesn't matter to me where I am. I seem to have
a gift for survival whether I like it or not. I might try
the farm for a while, but I refuse to dig ditches and
plant stuff and grub around. It's just not my thing."

"That's all right," said Oriana. "No one on the farm
has to do anything he doesn't want. How about you,
Wendy? It doesn't seem fair to desert you when you're
newly come to your independence."

"I might try the farm." Wendy was happily surprised
that Oriana would even think of asking her, especially
after her declaration that she was not a Den Mother.

She was also surprised at herself—to hear herself consider going. But what held her in Boston? Certainly not Peter Banbury and his ill-fated document. Maybe she was beginning to feel the same kind of admiration for Oriana and loyalty to her and her precepts that inspired Jez. And the farm sounded like an experience. Her curiosity was aroused. And, too, staying here might mean more encounters with Nell, as well as continual sad reminders of Donald.

"No one has to decide for another three days," said Oriana. "The rent's paid till then."

Wendy couldn't sleep. Her finger ached and her knee throbbed, and Jez had begun to wonder out loud if she shouldn't have taken Wendy to the Emergency Room for stitches, especially where a knee meant a hard place to heal. They all realized how upset and uncomfortable Wendy was, so they sat up talking with her, getting her cold drinks of fruit juice, and putting on records she wanted to hear. When at last she did fall asleep it was with a sense of belonging, as if she'd earned at last her way among friends. She also had definitely decided she would go to the farm for a few weeks. She did not want to give up and go home, not when she had found kindness and friendship and freedom. *And I'm not doing any harm*, she reassured herself. *Not to anyone. Not even to me.*

The next morning a sudden knocking at the door wakened them all. It was Peter Banbury. He came in quickly, shut the door, and sat on the couch by Wendy. His voice sounded urgent.

"Wendy, are you awake enough to talk?"

"There's nothing left to talk about, Peter. I haven't changed my mind at all about your document. The answer is still no."

"I agree with you. It wouldn't be successful. Besides, I'm afraid we have all the case history and pictures we need. Of someone else. Including a shot taken at the morgue this morning. I thought I'd come and mention it to you just in case any detectives come around later asking questions."

"What's happened?" Wendy yelped as she tried to pull herself up, and she hit her sprained finger, which was black and blue. She found she couldn't bend her knee at all.

"It seems the police fished a body out of the Charles this morning. It was a girl who used to be in one of Professor Zim's classes at Barnard, and he'd bumped into her here this summer and talked with her quite a lot. He couldn't believe the changes in her in just a year's time. She was colorful and she was around a lot. So he made notes on what she said about herself, about her life. And it turns out Zack had quite a few pictures of her. I'm afraid we've got all the case history we need."

"What was her name?" asked Wendy.

"Eleanor Norman. Late of Wampanagog, New York —a fashionable lake resort turned select suburb. She attended several top schools, traveled with her family, had everything she needed and more, too. Very brilliant. Graduated from high school at sixteen. Went to Barnard for a year. Dropped out. And last night, somehow or other, she ended up in the Charles."

"Why do you come to tell us?" Wendy asked. "It may mean you've got your bothersome case history accounted for. But I don't know any Eleanor Norman."

"Maybe we do," said Rolf. "Are you talking about Little Knocky Nell, as she has been known?"

"That's right," said Peter. "It's Nell."

"Oh—God!" Wendy choked. "Are you sure?"

"Zack was out taking early morning city pictures and was on the river bank when someone spotted a body floating and called the police. When they hauled her body out, Zack recognized her and phoned me. We got Professor Zim to identify her. Of course by the time Zack got to take pictures of her around here this summer and spring, the innocent-bird aspect had long since flown. But the facts on Nell make very convincing reading for a board of businessmen who can relate to her early background. It turns out a pretty grisly story, what?"

Wendy felt woozy and became very white, and Peter realized she had some cuts and bruises. "What happened to you last night, Wendy? Did a string on your lute snap and knock you out?"

"It's not funny, Peter. Actually—and this is so awful now—I had a fuss with Nell."

"What do you mean, Banbury, about if some detectives come around?" Rolf suddenly asked. "Wendy had nothing to do with Nell's ending up in the river."

"It's just that the police detectives we talked with when Professor Zim identified her were well acquainted with Nell. They've been on the Charles and Common squad this summer, and they knew she panhandled, and they knew she hung around with Donald. They knew Donald was booked for trespassing at this address and that he'd been sent to Waltham. They found Nell had been out there yesterday and raised hell. So they figured maybe she'd gone from a manic kind of state to a depressed state and thrown herself in the river last night. But there was some possibility she'd been beaten or hurt in an accident because of a bruise on her forehead. So they weren't sure whether she jumped in, fell in, or was pushed in. Due to her connection with Donald, and Donald's being picked up here, someone may come around and ask questions."

"We were all together last time we saw her—Jez and Rolf and I," said Wendy. "We watched her run out of sight. And she was headed toward the river. She had a kind of retreat—a place she liked—out on that Salt-and-Pepper Bridge. I wondered if she was going there. But that's all."

"What happened before that?"

Rolf told Peter what he and Jez had seen. Oriana added her impression that Nell had come and forced

Wendy to go with her. "I was really concentrating on other things, so what happened is only on the periphery of my mind," she explained. Jez remembered her suggestion to Nell that she might have a concussion and ought to go to the hospital.

While they were deciding whether to go to the police and volunteer the information or wait and see if anyone came to ask, the choice was taken from them. Two police detectives arrived, and identified themselves. So Wendy, Jez, and Rolf told the story of Nell as they knew it.

Wendy ended in tears. "I didn't hurt her!" she kept insisting. "She fell. But I didn't hurt her at all. And I wasn't responsible for Donald going to Waltham, either. It wasn't my fault!"

"Isn't this enough questioning?" Peter asked the officers. "I think Wendy's had a rough time here. She sounds a little hysterical to me."

"As long as you three were together, Miss Allardyce and Miss Peel and Mr. Snelson, when you last saw her, and you've been together ever since as you swear you have, I guess that's as helpful with your information as you can be. It seems like one of those indefinite things where unless someone actually saw her jump, we won't know if it was an accident or not. Of course, if she was under the influence of drugs, she may have jumped without intending to commit suicide. Well, thanks for your time."

Both men took rather a long look at each of them—at Rolf, with his Viking hair and his faded shirt and tight-topped jeans where even the little package of cigarette papers showed in outline in his pocket; at Jez, who tried to meet their eyes but couldn't hold the gaze, as she wondered if Mr. Volmarr discussed with the Charles Street squad any of the objects sold to him from her suitcase. They looked at Wendy and probably knew that while she protested she wasn't responsible, she was agonizing inside over whether she was. They didn't blink at Oriana in her purple tunic against her purple walls, but they filed it all away mentally.

"We'll check back with you all tomorrow, if we need anything more."

The men left. Oriana and Jez tried to comfort Wendy and stop her crying. Peter went practically to the kitchen and made a pitcher of very hot and black instant coffee for everyone. Finally Wendy controlled herself to an occasional gasp. But she was very distracted, only half listening as Rolf said, "They'll be back with a search warrant for sure."

"Why?" asked Jez. "There's nothing here of either Nell's or Donald's."

"No. But I could see the letters 'P-O-T' forming in their eyeballs. If they'd had a warrant, they would have raided us then."

"Then maybe I won't go to the farm!" said Oriana. "Maybe I'll let them arrest me. The laws are so ridiculous—all those penalties for possession of pot, or being in the presence of someone in possession of pot. Someone's got to change them."

"Does it *have* to be *you*, Oriana?" asked Peter wearily. "Couldn't you think just once of how your actions affect other people?"

"Who? My family? My father brought me up not to be a hypocrite. Now I'm not and he is."

"No—just all of you right here. This Nell thing is hard enough to sort out, without having you all picked up for possession, too. For once, Oriana, stop being pig-headed or pot-headed or whatever and listen to me. If you've got to make a test case out of your convictions, just don't do it here right now. Please."

"Peter," Wendy interrupted. "Is it *me* you're trying to protect from Captain Hooked and the Crocodile?"

"Yes."

"You mean you think one situation plus another situation blown up in the newspapers would add up to a big mess?"

"It very well could."

"I won't desert my friends."

"I didn't ask you to do that. I'm just asking Oriana to have her confrontation with the law at another time and another place. How about it, Oriana? I don't want to have to stamp on your sand castle."

"You always were a horrid little boy." But Oriana smiled when she said it. "I see your point, though, Peter. After all, I'm over twenty-one."

"And I'm not!" said Wendy. "Now you're deserting me."

"Not really. You can come to the farm. Or we can keep in touch. You don't ever really lose people you've known, Wendy."

Oriana's words made Wendy think of Donald, and that made her throat ache with the effort not to cry again. "Oh, I don't know!" she said impatiently. "I don't know what to do!"

"Drink your coffee," suggested Peter.

Oriana drank hers and didn't say anything for a while. Then she put her mug down and announced, "I dig the Peter Pan stuff, Peter. And if you want to keep this all like Never-Never Land for Wendy, I won't bring it crashing down to the Police Blotter of reality. In fact, I shall pack my Do-Not-Sell box and my poster and be off. Today."

"Don't do that on account of me," Wendy begged. "There I go again. Spoiling everything all around."

"I very rarely do anything that isn't exactly what I want to do," Oriana said. "So don't take this personally. Besides you knew anyway that I was planning to go. It was just a question of when." She stood on the couch, untaped the poster from the wall, and efficiently rolled it up. Wendy felt as if a staring eye had suddenly been closed.

Jez quietly collected records. Rolf went out to scrounge some cardboard cartons. Peter sat and watched Wendy, who stared sightlessly out at Sage Lane.

Oriana borrowed Peter's key to go below and phone the bus station for information. "While you're there, try South Station and see when there's a train through Westerly, Rhode Island," Peter told her.

"I'm going to the farm," said Wendy. "You can't make me go home."

"I'm not trying to make you go home. I'm just finding information in case you want it. What you do is up to you. I'll just say that it would take more courage and more guts to go home right now—than it would to escape reality some more at the farm."

"Maybe the farm isn't escape. Maybe it's very real."

"Quick! Before Oriana comes back—how real do you think William is?"

"Peter! Don't be nasty. Of course he's real."

"In his introverted, narrow way. He's doing his thing. Apparently everyone at the farm spends his time doing his own thing. But my question is: do you know what your own thing is, Wendy—so you can do it? Be honest."

"All right. I'll be honest. I'm not sure."

"Do you think you'll find it in another Never-Never Land like the farm? Or do you think you'll find it by going back home and graduating from the Nursery into the real world? The tough world. The everyday, commonplace world."

"But you're wrong there, Peter. After what's happened to Nell and to Donald, this now must be the tough world, the real world. Don't you see? Its realities were too much for them. You've got it the wrong way round. You call my home the Nursery. But I think my home is the Never-Never Land. All the unrealities I have to live with are at home. The conventions and the conformities. All the things I have to do at home that don't relate to life at all!"

"I wish I had my tape recorder, Wendy—just to play that one back and make you listen to yourself. Your home may not be ideal. Sure you want to change things. But isn't that the place to begin to work things out? Sure you can get along with people by drifting with them. When you're all drifting on a sea of pot it's gorgeously congenial. Great fun. No sweat. But the challenge—"

"Challenge is a dirty word," Wendy interrupted.

"I'll buy that. All right, the *point* in life is to live it thoroughly, use it—not escape from it. If you can't tell which is real and which is unreal, then it's too late. You're on the same road as Donald. And I'll go write up my lousy reports, and I'll file the Case History of Wendy A. in my heart under 'MM,' for Major Mistake. And I'll take the blame for it, too."

Peter looked as upset as he had when he'd discovered her in a fury over the document about herself. Wendy knew she'd succeeded in shooting him down, just as successfully as the Lost Boys shot Wendy in the play. But it didn't give her the satisfaction she'd expected. She only knew that just as Donald's and Nell's tragedies would always be the salt in her wounds, her reactions would irritate Peter's. *No one is really free,* she discovered.

Oriana came in with Rolf, who had rounded up five cartons from a grocery store. "The buses are impossible, and I can't hitchhike from Brattleboro to the farm anyway with a carton of records to carry. So I've hired a cab to drive us. Last fling of the old man's money, kiddies. We might as well enjoy it. The cabbie will be round in half an hour."

"What about Wendy's train?" asked Peter.

"One leaves at one o'clock."

"Well?" Peter asked Wendy.

"I don't know!" Wendy tried walking around, and her knee hurt so she had to sit down. The minute she sat, the cut cracked open and bled again. "What a mess.

If I go home this way, look at all the explaining I'll
have to do."

"Won't you anyway, if you go home?" asked Oriana.
"Parents expect explanations. Good ones. I really would
like to hear you explain Oriana Green, Jessie Peel, and
Ralph Snelson to your parents." She didn't particularly
mean to be sarcastic, but it came out that way.

"I wouldn't try to explain you to anyone," said
Wendy. "You don't have to explain your real friends."

"Don't go home, Wendy!" said Rolf. "You'll just be
back in the box with the lid on for another year."

Wendy didn't answer. She wanted to shut her eyes
and put her fingers in her ears and cut Oriana and Jez
and Rolf and Peter out of her presence while she tried
to think.

"I'm going downstairs before the suspense kills me,"
said Peter. "If you decide to go home, Wendy, I'll round
up a taxi to the station and go down on the train with
you to Westerly, if you want me to."

But Wendy made no reply. Jez squeezed her few
possessions into the suitcase along with whatever artifacts for sale were still in it. Rolf dismantled the record
player and its stereo speakers. Oriana rolled up the
crimson-dyed couch covers and stuffed them in boxes.

"I wonder what color the next tenant will paint this
place. Maybe chartreuse. Wouldn't that be horrible!"

Wendy gave up trying to think or to reason. She
could make long mental lists of pros and cons, about
going to the farm. She could flip a coin. She could pray
—for guidance from the Fickle Finger of Fate. Or whatever. She could say "Om" over and over, and see what
peaceful revelation—if any—ended up in her mind. She
felt unhappy and tortured and miserable. Was going
home growing up, or giving in? Was going to the farm
escaping from, or to, reality? "I always knew I had a
messy mind!" she suddenly burst out. "But now I don't
think I have any mind at all."

The doorbell rang. Oriana buzzed and opened the door. From below, a man yelled up, "Taxi!"

"Well, Wendy. This is it. Are you coming?" asked Rolf.

Wendy looked from face to face. At Jez, who had started out suspicious and aggressive and ended being tender and kind. At Oriana, who certainly marched to her own inner music and made Wendy wish she could hear it clearly, too. At Rolf, existing in his own way of escape. She knew each of them had come to some understanding of himself, for better or worse. The better or worse depended on how you saw life. And she suddenly knew she hadn't come to her own understanding yet. She'd begun. But she had a long way to go.

"I'm afraid I'm going home after all. Back in the box, Rolf. But with some windows cut out and a door or two opened."

She stood up. "Thank you, Oriana. And Jez. And you, Rolf. Don't forget me. It's been real! Despite what Peter says about that. Very, very real."

Oriana and Jez accepted her decision without any comment, and even Rolf said, "Well—to each his own thing," although his disappointment was obvious. They all kissed each other goodby, and Wendy hastily wrote her address at Meridian Farm and made them promise to keep in touch. Then they picked up their cartons and went down the stairs. She heard the taxi doors slam and the car drive away.

She sat painfully down on the hassock, which Oriana hadn't bothered to take, and felt too empty to cry.

When Peter ran up and found her still there, he looked tremendously relieved, but he thoughtfully refrained from any editorial comment. He fastened her lute case, and helped her stuff her things into the rucksack. He helped her downstairs, found a cab, and they made the train just in time.

Luckily they got a double seat so she could put her

knee out straight. But compared to the happy excitement Wendy had felt on the way to Boston, this made a somber ride.

"I'd like to go home with you, Wendy, and see your family," Peter said, as she spotted landmarks approaching Westerly. "It might help ease the way."

"Oh, Peter. I don't know. This just has to be something I do myself and get it over with and then go on from there. I think right now, my parents wouldn't see beyond your beard. You'd just confuse the issue. Just as you confuse me. I still think you were wrong, wrong, wrong—using me as you did. But maybe what you're trying to do is right. I guess there are—some kids—who need help."

"Just let the feeling grow on you," said Peter. "But I won't come with you now. Here's money for a cab, though. You can't hike two miles on that knee."

"But I owe you a lot of money already."

"Don't sweat it. I'll shave my beard and come collect the money next week, if you like. But I refuse to part with my sideburns."

"I don't really care what you do," said Wendy. But as she said it, she realized that wasn't true. "Well—come and collect the money. But don't shave the beard. If that's your real self."

"It's the real me. Wendy, don't you think if Peter Pan's been around all these years, he'd have grown a beard by now?"

"Wester-LY-WEST-erly." The train stopped. Peter helped her down the steps, waved up a taxi for her, and leaped back on board the train as it pulled out. He had decided to go on to New York.

The taxi driver stuck her lute upright on the back seat so it looked like another person sitting there. "Two miles out on the Post Road," Wendy said. "Meridian Farm."

She still hadn't thought of what to say when she got there, and driving the two miles made them speed by.

She stopped the cab at the end of the drive, just so she'd have that much more time to figure out the right line for an entrance. What if no one were home? That would be the anticlimax of her life—like the lights going out at the dinner table during her speech for freedom.

But as she came near the house, she could see the car by the garage. The door to her father's studio was open, which meant he was working but not against a deadline, so he could be disturbed. She could hear the boys shouting from the Wallow. A big patch of towel down on the far corner of the green lawn caught her eye. Rosalyn and Annetta were lying there, glistening with suntan lotion. She could hear the FM radio in the kitchen encouraging her mother to accomplish the domestic chores to music.

They aren't missing me at all! thought Wendy. She had pictured them in a line by the front door, white and weeping and gnashing their teeth. *Nothing's changed! I can't stand it! I'll look under the shingles and find that terrible oath in blood saying "I'll never grow up," and I'll burn it up and I'll sneak away again, and they'll never know how I came back—and their cold indifference drove me away.* If she hadn't been carrying the lute and the rucksack she would have made an elocutionary gesture. *I'll win the Elsie L. Fribble Prize for sure!*

But she opened the screen door, put her things down, and yelled, "Hey! I'm home!"

It was hardly the line she'd intended. But it would do for an opener.

Today's
Hangups
and the
Generation
Gap

I'm really dragged but nothing gets me down

by Nat Hentoff
author of *Jazz Country*

Jeremy Wolf is a high school senior whose
soul is torn between his responsibility to his
country and his social existence. With wit and
with rare understanding, this novel examines
both sides of the generation gap.

"A taut, highly articulate exposition of today's
hangups . . ."—*The Virginia Kirkus Service*

". . . timely and important . . ."
—*The New York Times*

A LAUREL-LEAF BOOK   60c

If you cannot obtain copies of this title from your local bookseller, just
send the price (plus 15c per copy for handling and postage) to Dell Books,
Post Office Box 1000, Pinebrook, N. J. 07058. No postage or handling charge
is required on any order of five or more books.

TUNED OUT

A Novel by Maia Wojciechowska
Winner of the 1965 Newbery Medal

Summer turns into a nightmare for sixteen-year-old Jim when his brother Kevin comes home from college. Kevin, whom Jim idolizes, has changed drastically during his year away. He has become a person full of doubts, with urgent needs—one of which is drugs.

We share the experience of that terrible summer in this moving book—the LSD and marijuana, the hippies, the disillusionment, the helpless confusion and fear. It is all recorded frankly, to the final horror of Kevin's freaking out and the shaky beginnings of his redemption.

"No recent novel or factual treatment succeeds as well in showing the self-deception, the sense of alienation, the bitterness against the established order today . . ."
—*The Horn Book Magazine*

A LAUREL-LEAF BOOK   50c